The Ghost Files

Volume 4 - Part 2

By Apryl Baker

The Ghost Files

Copyright © 2017 by Apryl Baker.
All rights reserved.
Second Print Edition: August 2018

Limitless Publishing, LLC
Kailua, HI 96734
www.limitlesspublishing.com

Formatting: Limitless Publishing

ISBN-13: 978-1-64034-993-3

Dedication

For Janna

Prelude

November 3, 1862

The soft glow of evening light bathes my face while the sweet smell of homemade apple pie draws me to the front door of the dilapidated farmhouse. A lone barn stands in the distance with horses grazing in the paddock. The wood floors are smooth, a stark contrast to the peeling wallpaper and cracked ceilings. The stairwell on the right is well worn, a lifetime of feet having traveled it.

It's cold, the shadows flickering across the walls as I move deeper into the house. I glance behind me, the fading light of the sun echoing in the deepening darkness of the house. I don't want to be

1

in here, but I can't make myself turn around and leave. There is nowhere else to go.

The kitchen is at the very back of the house, its entrance an archway. An older woman stands at the kitchen counter, her back to me as she kneads dough. Two apple pies rest on another counter. The rich, sweet smell of cinnamon calls out to my empty stomach. It has been ages since we feasted on such treats.

"Don't just stand there, Abagail. Come help me clean up this mess."

My grandmother sounds impatient, and I falter, not used to hearing her snap at me so. "Girl, I got no time for your foolishness. Now get in here and start cleaning!"

The irritation in the older woman's voice lights a fire under me, and I move to the sink. Steaming hot water waits in a cracked bowl. I start to fill it with the various dishes, surreptitiously looking around. A soup pot simmers on the old coal and wood stove, the heady scent of roasting lamb wafting up to tease my senses. It is my favorite, but surely we can't afford such an extravagance. We need all the sheep for the wool we can sell. Gran hands me an apron to put on over my simple dress, much like the one she herself wears.

"The Reverend came by today."

The Reverend? A sense of dread settles heavily in my heart. "What did he want?"

"He's looking for a wife."

A wife. Panic chokes me and I can't breathe, but I keep washing dishes.

"He knows we don't have much to offer him but the farm, but he's willing to marry you despite that."

The dish I'm holding falls from my numb hands, splintering when it hits the hard wood planks. Terror rises up, washing out every other sound or emotion. He wants to marry me?

The crash makes Gran whirl around, shock bleeding to anger on her face. "You foolish girl. Look what you have done! We don't have many plates left after having to sell them off."

"I am sorry."

My grandmother shakes her head. "Pick this mess up, and then go get yourself cleaned up. The Reverend will be here for supper."

Tonight? He is coming tonight? Those thoughts swirl through my mind. I bend and start collecting the pieces of glass. My first thought is to reason with Gran, but I dismiss the idea. The old woman has worked hard to keep us safe, fed, and with a roof over our heads. She's getting on in years, in her sixties. To her, this offer of marriage would be a gift from God.

But God has nothing to do with Reverend Aaron Whitmore.

The man is evil. Full of rage and hatred.

My friend, Kaitlin, refused to marry him. He declared she was possessed by demons. Her parents, being the pious people they are, agreed to take her to the church to let the good Reverend cleanse her of the Devil's grip. They left her with him for a week.

When she came home, she wasn't the same. The once vibrant girl, full of life and joy, became timid, scared of her own shadow. She shrank into herself. The

Reverend withdrew his offer of marriage, claiming he couldn't knowingly enter a union with someone who had been unclean.

Kaitlin finally confessed to me what happened during her week with the Reverend. He tied her up, he beat her, he raped her. All to cleanse the evil from her body. He tortured her because she refused to marry him.

What man of God would take his anger out on such an innocent girl?

I begged Kaitlin to tell her parents, but she refused. Reverend Whitmore had told her he'd deny it all and tell them she hadn't been purified. That he'd take her back to the church and invite her father along to witness the cleansing. It would be a true cleansing. The type of torture they'd put so many women through during the witch trials.

I stand, depositing the glass in the bin used to collect what little trash we accumulated. I'd dispose of it later, when it got a little fuller. Without a word to my grandmother, I turn and leave the kitchen. When I enter my room at the top of the stairs, I close the door and lean against it.

I try to fight through the chaos of my own thoughts, to make some sense of what Gran has just told me. She's handing me over to the Devil himself, and there isn't anything I can do or say to convince her otherwise. Reverend Whitmore has them all fooled. Including my grandmother.

Kaitlin had been right, I realize. Her parents *wouldn't* have believed her. They are deeply religious and put all their trust and faith in a man who is supposed to represent the will of God.

The will of God. A hollow laugh follows the thought. I can't believe it is God's will to put me into the hands of someone like Reverend Whitmore. How could it be God's will to make us so poor we almost starved to death last winter? God has no part of this.

I grew up in the church, listening to Gran preach about faith. Despite her ironclad belief in God, sometimes I have questions. I don't understand how God can be such a kind and forgiving entity, but make us suffer so much. Tests, Gran calls all our misfortune. A test of strength and determination on our part.

I'm not strong enough to withstand the test of Reverend Whitmore. My fear pulses on such a deep level, it's almost a physical pain when I think about life with him.

The curtains flutter in the cooling breeze. The letter opener on the desk beneath it holds my attention. Thoughts I never thought I'd have start to confuse me, but I'm terrified of doing nothing and letting God's will, as Gran would say, decide my fate.

Last winter I found a book in the attic when I went searching for extra blankets. An old leather-bound journal. A journal I'd read late at night, burning candles we couldn't afford to replace, but I'd done it anyway. It described the life of a woman who'd had everything she'd ever desired, and that journal held all her secrets.

I often wonder if they are the ravings of a madwoman or the true life and times of a brilliant, independent woman. The things she'd done to achieve her goals make me shudder to think about, but in this moment, the idea of being given to the Reverend terrifies me just a little more.

Without hesitation, I go to my closet and dig the book out from where I'd hidden it. I know what I'm about to do, what it might cost me in the end, but anything has to be better than becoming the property of Reverend Whitmore. Even death would be better than that.

I smile triumphantly when I pull the book from behind a stack of old linens on the top shelf. My hands tremble, but I refuse to think about the consequences of my actions. It simply could be the ravings of a madwoman, so best not to let myself worry until there's a reason to worry. Still, I lock the door and light the oil lamp before opening the book to the summoning ritual.

The design is intricate, and I study it before attempting to draw it on a piece of paper. After several test runs, I nod. I can draw it. Closing my eyes, I send up a silent prayer asking for forgiveness for what I'm about to do. I'm honestly not sure if there is a God, but just in case, I want Him to understand I have no choice left to me. Trusting in prayer isn't going to fix this dilemma. I won't be sold off to someone that even the Devil himself would hide from.

I pick up the letter opener and stand, moving to the center of the room. My hand quivers when I open my left palm, the letter opener clutched in my right. I hesitate, my grandmother's voice booming a warning in my mind, and I know I should listen to that voice. What I'm about to do...I will probably never even begin to understand what it's going to cost me.

I'm not prepared when the blade comes down and slices across my palm. A whimper escapes my lips at the sharp sting of the fresh wound. I'd cut deep, the blood pooling immediately. I drop to my knees, doing all I can to not panic, to convince myself I'm not being foolish. I'm fighting to live. My finger dips into the blood, and I begin to draw.

When the drawing is complete, I stand and utter the words that will bring the demon to me.

"Conjuro te mihi facere iussus dimittere te donec. Venite ad me!"

Which basically calls a demon to do my bidding until I release it.

Nothing happens. Why didn't it work? Maybe the book really is the writings of an old crazy woman. Disappointment weighs heavily on my heart. What am I to do now?

I fall to the floor, the wetness of tears beginning to stream down my face. I can't marry him. I can't.

A hand smooths down my hair and I fall back, startled. My mouth opens in a silent O when I see the man standing over me. I'm shocked, and a tiny flutter starts in my stomach while I drink in every detail of him. He's beautiful. Long, dark hair, strong cheekbones, and his eyes are amber, like the wolves that constantly prowl the farm. I feel an instant attraction to him, and the depth and intensity of it frightens me perhaps more so than my fear of the good Reverend.

"Come, child." He holds out his hand, and I take it. Heat, hotter than any flame I've ever beheld, blazes like a wildfire across my skin at his simple touch. His smile is kind when he helps me to my feet then walks me to my bed, where I sit. I can't stop staring at him. He's…he's the most handsome man I've ever seen.

"I didn't think it worked," I murmur, twisting my hands.

"It didn't." He cups my face, and I can't break my gaze from him.

"But…"

"Shhh," he hushes me. "I heard you and came to see if I may be of assistance. What is it you require that you would summon a demon?"

"Are you…a…"

"A demon?"

I nod, my voice abandoning me when his fingers stroke my cheek.

"Yes, I am. Does that frighten you?"

I shake my head. Not if he can save me from the Reverend.

"It should."

A quiver of fear runs down my spine. The ice in his eyes belies the warmth of his voice. I begin to understand the mistake I made in calling out to something as evil, or perhaps even more so than the Reverend. What have I done?

"Tell me why you need the services of a demon, girl. My patience grows weary."

"I do not wish to marry a man my grandmother has chosen for me."

A laugh rumbles out of him, and it is every bit as beautiful as he. But deadly. There is a dark bite to it. When he steps away from me, I can breathe for the first time since he entered my room.

"It cannot be so bad that you'd trade your soul to escape it."

My voice is strong, despite the terror beginning to overtake me. I'd read that journal carefully. "It's not just any man I am escaping. The Reverend Whitmore is evil."

His eyes go distant, and they swirl with a thousand thoughts all at once. When he blinks, for only a moment, those amber orbs have gone black, a ring of yellow where the iris should be. If I had blinked, I would have missed it.

"Ah, I know Reverend Aaron Whitmore. He and I shall see each other soon enough."

There is a finality in his voice. Evil knows evil.

"I won't marry him." I make my resolve heard in my voice. I will escape the man, no matter what I must do to accomplish it.

The demon cocks his head. "You could flee now, child. Why ask me for help?"

"Because I don't want to *just* flee." I wring my hands again. "I don't want to ever be in this position again. I want to be strong, powerful, a force no man will ever take advantage of."

"You seek power and position." He strokes his chin, regarding me like one would a horse they are considering purchasing. "And if I told you I could give you all this, make your dreams a reality, what would you give me for it?"

"Anything."

The smile that lights up his face is full of dark promises. "And if I said the price was your soul? An eternity of belonging to me?"

"If you can give me everything I want, then, yes, you can have my soul."

He squats in front of me, his amber

eyes piercing. "I do have plans for you, my beautiful child. Plans that will thwart a plot against me."

"I don't understand."

He smiles. "You don't need to, child. All you have to do is serve me, and I will give you the world. Do you agree? Your soul in exchange for everything you could ever want?"

"I do." There is no hesitation this time. The words are spoken with a clarity I didn't know I possessed. This is my only way out. At least the only way out I can see.

A parchment appears in his hand, a quill pen in the other, which I take. He nods to my still bleeding palm, and I dip the pen in the blood, signing my name to the bottom of the contract. I don't read it. There's no need.

"Very, very good, my child. I shall take you to a friend in New Orleans who will become your family. She'll teach you all the ways of witchcraft, and she'll introduce you to society. You will have everything you desire."

Joy surges in my heart as I gaze up at

my savior.

"Now, child. You need a new name. What shall we call you?"

The sweetest smile tips my lips. "Tara."

Chapter One

~*Mattie*~

Today is Meg's funeral.

I slip into my black flats and adjust the simple black dress I'm wearing. The severe bun I've put my dark hair up in is one Meg taught me. My breath catches as a new wave of grief smashes into me. I still can't believe she's gone. There are no tears, only a staggering pain in my heart. I hated her the tiniest bit because she lied to me, but I loved her. She was my best friend, and now she's dead.

Because of me.

Mattie Louise Hathaway. The harbinger of bad luck. Me in a nutshell.

My foster sister, Mary Cross, knocks

on the door and breezes in. Her long blonde hair is pulled back, making her look even paler against the dark gray woolen dress she keeps tugging at. She hates the thing because it's itchy, but she said it is the only dress she has suitable for a funeral. Mary didn't really know Meg, but she knows me and Dan, so she's going to support us. It's what sisters do, she said. I'm grateful every day for her. Blood sisters we may not be, but she *is* my sister in every way that counts. We chose each other, and that bond can sometimes be even stronger than blood.

"Dan's on his way." She sits in my desk chair, her eyes zeroing in on me. "You ready for this?"

Is anyone ever ready to say goodbye to someone they love? "No, but we'll get through it."

Mary fusses with her hair while I make a point of staring down at my shoes. We're both somber today. I've never been to a funeral, not even my mom's. She'd been buried while I was still in the hospital recovering from her attack on me. I'm not sure what to expect, other than what I've seen on TV. Those are always somber affairs. So I guess we're at least in the right frame of mind.

I haven't talked to Mary about her run-in with Deleriel yet. I didn't get back here until late last night because I'd been visiting with the grandparents the last few days. I need to speak to her soon, though. We need to get out in front of this before Deleriel decides to make a move. He's a fallen angel who eats the souls of little children, and he's got his heart set on taking Mary back to hell with him. So not gonna happen.

I'm still vexed she didn't tell me about it. I had to hear about it from Silas, a demon who claims to be my great something-or-other grandfather. His last visit dropped the proverbial ton of bricks into my lap with all his secrets, secrets involving me that I haven't come to terms with yet. Silas terrifies me to begin with, but if everything he told me is true, I'm going to need his help with Deleriel. Not something I'm looking forward to.

We are both startled by a horn outside. Dan's here. I get up and follow Mary out of the house. We pause on the porch and look at the empty yard beside ours. The Burnette house stands next to us like a giant black shadow, ready to exhale its sorrow any moment.

Mr. Burnette's seven-year-old granddaughter, Kayla, went missing a few days ago. She's the latest in a long line of children who went missing in the Charlotte area. Those kids turned up dead a week after they disappeared. We suspect they are victims of Deleriel. If he has Kayla, God only knows the horrors that poor little girl is going through.

"Come on, Mattie." Mary tugs at my arm, snapping my attention back to her. "It's time to go."

Dan's father is driving us. He's wearing a nice black suit, and Dan is sitting in the front seat, staring straight ahead, his face as empty as a barren wasteland. Mary and I pile in the back seat, and we head to the cemetery without a word. No one is in the mood to talk.

The drive to Old Settlers' Cemetery in Charlotte flies by. Before I know it, Mr. Richards is parking the car and getting out. Dan and I sit there, even after Mary's gotten out. Neither of us is ready for this. He's still staring straight ahead, silent, and I'm worried about him. He hasn't even processed his grief. There's been no time, what with Kayla missing. Dan's thrown himself into finding her. He has whiteboards set up at Zeke's. He's very good at what he does, but if his captain finds out, he might lose his job. She's still pissed at him for poking his nose in the case that ended up with Meg being shot and killed.

"We have to get out, you know," I say softly.

"I know."

After a full minute, I prod him again. "Dan."

"I know!" The words come out in an explosion, one I didn't expect, but fully understand. He takes a deep breath. "I know."

His dad knocks on the window, and I shake my head at him. Despite what I said, we'll sit here for as long as Dan needs to. Mr. Richards frowns, clearly concerned about his son, but he walks away. Dan needs a minute or ten to get out of the car.

"I don't know if I can do it." His voice is hollow, empty. "How can I face her father? I was right there. I could have stopped it somehow…"

"No, Dan, you couldn't have stopped it." I will not let him blame himself. I am the only one who should shoulder this blame. "You weren't even there when he took us. You couldn't have stopped it."

"If I had died, she would have been safe, like the angel said. She'd have been home grieving."

"Yeah, that's true enough, but you're forgetting one thing, Dan." I lean forward, my lips by his ear. "Paul was obsessed with her. That was no one's fault. Stalkers, especially the psychotic ones, they don't stop. He would have taken her eventually, and her death would have been messy, full of humiliation and pain. You remember what he did to those other girls. They were practice runs for him. Can you imagine everything she would have suffered? Yes, the angel was right in that she died because *you* lived, but he didn't say anything about the type of death she would have suffered if you had died. You saved her from that, Dan."

It was something I'd thought a lot about. Yes, we had bucked fate and caused all sorts of problems when I refused to let Dan die and he chose to stay for me, but no one even considered the good things that decision might bring about. Meg's death was quick. If she'd been kidnapped by Paul and held hostage? Another story altogether. That's what I choose to believe. I only hope Dan can do the same. He needs to so he doesn't blame himself anymore. I hate what it's doing to him.

"Do you really believe that?" His words are halted, unsteady.

"Yeah, Officer Dan, I really believe that. You saved her from a fate worse than the death she received. I believe she'd thank you for sparing her that."

His bows his head and a shudder goes through him. "I just want her to know how sorry I am. That I didn't mean for her to die."

"She knows, Dan."

"How can you be so sure?"

"I'm the Ghost Girl, remember?" I try for a joke, but it falls flat. "Trust me, if she blamed either of us, her ghost would be here, blistering us both with that vengeful tongue of hers. The girl could hold a grudge like nobody's business. That's not the case, though. She's not here because her soul crossed over. She had no unfinished business. She's at peace, so let her memory stay at peace. She loved you, and that's all you need to hold on to."

A sigh so deep it could hold the sorrows of every broken heart ripples through him. His hand reaches back for mine, and I take it. He holds it so tight it hurts, but I only grip it back. "Thank you, Squirt."

"You're welcome, Officer Dan."

"I think I'm ready to go now."

He lets go of my hand, and we get out of the car. Dan takes my hand again and we walk over to where Mary and his father stand waiting. He holds onto me like a lifeline. This is what we do. When one of us hurts, the other is there, ready to help ease the pain. It's what we'll *always* do.

The cemetery is old, dating as far back as 1776, and it's smack in the middle of the city. It's one of the few places I've never visited. Ghosts tend to hang around cemeteries, and I refuse to go anywhere I might get overwhelmed.

Except today. Because it's for Megan. And Dan needs me.

As soon as we step on the path leading into the maze of gravestones, I hear them. They batter at me like the wind does a shutter during a storm, a constant banging inside my head. Thanks to that tattoo Caleb had given me in New Orleans, they can't overwhelm me anymore. In fact, they are muted, but there are so many it doesn't matter. It's like a pressure swelling inside my head. I blink and keep my attention focused on the ground beneath me, putting one foot in front of the other.

The warm summer day turns colder as the dead press in, surrounding us. Several people shiver, but they don't pay attention. They can't see what I see.

There are Civil War era soldiers lounging against headstones, their wounds evident and glaring. Others are ghosts who died of natural causes, and some are horrific, having suffered gruesome deaths. They are from all walks of life, from every era of history that marks the myriad of headstones on these hallowed grounds.

These ghosts are harmless. Sad, lonely—lost, even—but harmless. It's the ones crowded around outside the gates that have me unnerved. There is a malignancy there, a darkness that surrounds them. These are the dangerous ones, the ones who are as vicious in death as they were in life, and others who went mad from being here too long and letting their anger at being dead fester within them.

We follow Mary and Mr. Richards to some empty seats and sit. Mr. Johnson, Meg's dad and the current mayor of Charlotte, sits in the front row, staring blankly at his daughter's coffin. We're on the opposite side, near the front, so I have a clear view of him. Part of me wants to go over and say something. He was always so nice to me. The other part of me is saying to stay as far away from him as I can. I'm probably the last person he wants to see. I lived, and his daughter died. How can I look him in the eyes? How can he not blame me for that?

The minister starts the service, and I tune it out, the ghosts pressing in tighter, trying to force me to talk to them. They know I can hear them. Ghosts are the worst gossips, and they've spread the word about my abilities. Most times it's easy to ignore them, but when I'm surrounded by a small horde of them, it's harder. They are intent on getting my attention, and their cries pound into my head like a jackhammer. The pain is so intense it's almost debilitating.

One gets right in my face, his green eyes penetrating. He'd been in some kind of accident when he died. I can see the seatbelt bruise clearly across his shirtless chest. His stomach has a large, black bruise covering most of his lower abdomen. Aside from some cuts and scrapes on his face, he looks unharmed. Internal bleeding. Has to be.

Ignore him and he'll go away. I chant this over and over and focus instead on the minister. He's tall, skinny, maybe in his sixties. I squint, trying to pay attention to him and not the guy shouting obscenities at me no one else can hear. That's when I notice this haze around him. It's dark, like a cloud obscuring everything else. I tilt my head, studying it. Cancer. He has cancer. Maybe six months left because he doesn't know he has it.

Wait…what the heck? I know he has cancer and exactly six more months to live. Exactly. Fudgepops. I shouldn't know that, but I do. Why do I know that?

Someone waves at me from behind the minister, and to my shock, it's Reaper Boy. The one who tried to take Dan from me and later helped me navigate the Between, the realm separating this life and the next. It's chock full of nasty beasties waiting to gobble up lost souls.

He crooks his finger at me and motions for me to join him. I shake my head. Not in the middle of Meg's funeral. I will not let ghosty things make me disturb the service and further upset Dan or Mr. Johnson.

My hands clench when a burst of pain knifes through my head, drawing out a whimper. I bite my lip and glance at Dan, who doesn't seem to have heard. He's staring at Meg's coffin, his eyes almost frigid. Odd. He seems more angry than sad.

Mary leans over, her head nearly against mine. "I hear them too."

I jerk my head around, my eyes wide. "Does it hurt?"

She shakes her head. "It's more like a loud buzz, or white noise. Annoying, but it doesn't hurt."

Mary garnered the ability to hear ghosts after she spent so much time on the ghost plane last year. She'd been kidnapped by my then foster mother and tortured for weeks. Her soul traveled to me, and with Dan's help, we were able to save her. I ended up one of Mrs. Olson's victims in the process. Surviving that ordeal is one of the things we share, one of the things that makes us family now.

The crowd standing pulls my attention

back to the service. It's time to throw the flowers in the grave. Long-stemmed white roses. Meg loved them more than any other flower. We'd been handed one on our way to our seats earlier. I look at the one I have clutched in my hand, the thorns biting into my skin. It's not until I see the blood seeping down my palm that I feel the pain. Hissing, I relax my hand. Several of them had pierced my skin, and there is blood everywhere. Dang it.

I grit my teeth and stand, filing along behind the other people. This has never made sense to me. What purpose do flowers in a grave serve? Meg's ghost isn't even here to see it. It's a pointless tradition.

Not so pointless if you understand the why of it.

I stumble at the words. I glance to the side and see one of the Civil War soldiers walking along beside me. His golden hair is matted with blood near the back, and a gaping hole is torn clean through his shoulder, the cloth of his gray uniform jacket blackened around the edges where the bullet went in. A Confederate soldier.

You can hear me? I keep the conversation quiet. Now is not the time to be talking to myself out loud.

Yes, ma'am. His chuckle vibrates along my self-consciousness.

Is there something you need?

No, ma'am, but I suspect you need me.

What? Why would you think that?

You are here to mourn, and you should be able to do that in peace.

I realize the ghosts have gone quiet. Not even a whisper. I still see the grouchy one who'd been all up in my face, but he's at a respectful distance. When had that happened? This soldier chased them away. I stare up at him, shocked, but appreciative.

Thank you.

He nods and keeps walking beside me as we get closer to the open grave. They've already lowered her into the ground. I can't slow down, or I would. I don't want to see it. To see her down there in the earth. I know it's just a shell, but I can't shake this awful feeling. She hated cold, dark places. It doesn't seem right to put her body there.

When I step up and look down, my breath catches. The silver coffin sits at the bottom, several dozen flowers already littering the top and the ground around it. This isn't right. A tear rolls down my cheek. It isn't right. I close my eyes, and a vision of her laughing blue eyes greets me. She should be here, torturing me with trips to the mall. None of this is fair.

A hand comes down on my shoulder, and I blink. Mr. Johnson is standing beside me, his blue eyes wide with grief and pain, but not angry. His arm slides around my shoulder, and he pulls me into a hug.

"I'm so sorry, Mr. Johnson."

"Megan loved you like her own sister, Mattie." His words are heavy, his voice wrought with a cascade of tears. "She was so happy when she came home and told me the two of you were friends again. I've never seen her that happy."

"I…"

"You blame yourself for her death." His arm tightens around me. "I can see it in your face, but, Mattie, it wasn't your fault. The blame lies with a very disturbed young man."

Paul Owens was definitely a disturbed young man. The younger brother of my ex-boyfriend, Jake, Paul was obsessed with Meg, as well as having an unhealthy need to hurt and kill women. He'd killed his brother that night. While Jake's soul had gone on, his body remained alive. I'd been able to put Eric's soul in his body, giving the Owens family back one son, while giving my ghost friend another chance at a life stolen from him.

"I'm sorry too, Mr. Johnson." Dan appears in front of us. "I wish I could have done something, gotten there sooner…"

"None of that." Mr. Johnson cuts him off. "You shouldn't even have been out of the hospital, young man. What you did was more than enough. You tried to save her, and that's all that counts. Neither of you is responsible for her death. I want you to go on with your lives, be happy for her. It's what she would have wanted."

He gives me another hug and shakes Dan's hand. Mr. Richards pushes us along. We're holding up the line. I toss the rose into the grave and let him herd us away from the gravesite. My mind is still reeling. I would have wagered everything I own on the fact Meg's dad blamed us for her death. But he doesn't. How is that possible?

"I need a minute." I stop walking when we're away from the others, but not outside the gates. There's someone I need to speak with. "I...I need a minute by myself, okay?"

Dan's eyes zero in on me. "What's wrong?"

"Nothing." Well, if you count Reaper Boy as nothing. He's patiently waiting down by this big, ancient-looking crypt. "I just need a minute, okay?"

"I'll wait for her, Dad. You and Mary go on to the car." He waits for them to leave then turns to me. "Spill."

Dan's not buying my story for a hot minute. I can see it in his eyes.

"I need to talk to the reaper before we leave." My hand automatically comes up and covers my mouth. I hadn't meant to tell him that. I never could lie to him, though. It's those big old puppy dog eyes of him.

His face pales. "Reaper?"

It's why I hadn't wanted to tell him. He'd just survived a reaping, barely. If it hadn't been for Silas hiding him, I'm not sure I could have saved him from death.

"What's he want?"

"I don't know. I haven't talked to him yet."

"Is it safe?" His gaze sweeps the cemetery, but he can't see him. He doesn't need to know it's the same reaper who came for him the first time. It would only upset him.

"Yeah, he's the one who saved me from the little soulless monster in the morgue. He's not going to hurt me. I'll be fine, I promise."

His eyes narrow, but he nods. "Want me to come with?"

"No." Absolutely not. No sense in tempting fate. Especially around a reaper who should have reaped Dan's soul to begin with. "I won't be long. Just stay here."

I'll guard him, ma'am.

I nod to the soldier, thankful. I don't think any of the ghosts here within the gates are vengeful, but you never know.

I pick my way down the hill carefully. I'm only wearing two-inch heels, but I'm clumsy, and falling down a hill is not on my to-do list for today.

"Took you long enough." He's grouchy. Not my problem.

"I was at a funeral, in case you didn't notice."

"I don't like graveyards." He's also nervous. Why hadn't I noticed?

"Why?"

"Why what?"

"Why don't you like graveyards?" Seriously, he's a reaper. Graveyards should be his favorite spot.

"They're unnerving."

"Isn't this like a smorgasbord to a reaper?" I wave at the souls waiting to descend upon me the minute the soldier removes his protection.

"No, Mattie, graveyards are unnatural." He shifts from foot to foot, his fingers twitching.

"Unnatural?"

"It's not only the souls of the dead that reside here, little reaper." He flashes me a smile, but his eyes are dark, full of an alien fear I don't understand.

"What did you want?" If he's afraid of this place, I'm not going to stand here all day. I'm out.

"I sensed your unease. Something to do with your reaping ability. Remember I am assigned to guide you. When something new happens, I know it. What did you experience?"

"The minister." That has to be what he's talking about. I explain what happened earlier, and he nods slowly.

"What you saw was a death knell. A shroud, if you will, but you shouldn't have been able to see it."

I tilt my head, but he answers the question before I can ask it.

"That is the ability of a full-blown reaper. One who has died and assumed their responsibilities. You're a living reaper. Your job is only to assist in convincing the lost in crossing over. It's an amazing feat that you can even open the doorway that leads to the hall where we navigate them through the Between. You shouldn't be able to do it. There's not a living reaper in our known history who had that ability."

I have no idea how to respond to that.

"No wonder they wanted a guide assigned to you," he mutters. "You shouldn't be able to do even a tenth of what you can. Your abilities are growing at an alarming rate."

"That's a bad thing?"

He throws his hands up, frustrated. "I don't know."

The crypt door behind us creaks, and we both freeze.

Laughter echoes inside the dark entrance of the now open crypt.

Just as I turn to run, something snakes out, grabs my arm, and drags me inside, the door slamming shut behind me.

Leaving me in the dark.

Only I'm not alone.

Chapter Two

Crap, crap, crap.

Leave it me to get trapped in a crypt with no cell phone. Not that I have any hope of getting service behind the heavy stone walls, but at least I could have used the flashlight app.

It's darker than the blackest of night in here, and it stinks to high heaven. More than that, I can hear *something* scuttling around in the dark. It has to be rats. They love places like this. I have bigger problems than rats at the moment, though.

The laugh I'd heard earlier whispers around me. No more creepy children, please. Not here in the dark.

Someone's banging on the door, so I

know they're trying to find a way to get me out. Dan won't leave me in here. He knows how I feel about small, dark places…places where I'm trapped with no way out. My captivity at the hands of Mrs. Olson still gives me nightmares. He won't leave me here. *Please don't leave me in here.*

Steps sound to my left, and I whirl in that direction, fighting the uncontrollable panic trying to bubble up at the memories of my time with Mrs. Olson. Where is it? It's either one of those little yellow-eyed demonic children or one of the things Reaper Boy was talking about. He said it wasn't only ghosts that resided in cemeteries. All those horror movies I've watched are haunting me now. I keep imagining ghouls, monstrous creatures that burrow through a maze of tunnels beneath us then through the graves, eating the rotting flesh of the decaying corpses.

Stop it. This isn't helping. I will get out. Dan knows I'm in here. I am not strapped to a chair in a basement with a crazy lady intent on doing me harm with no hope of rescue. Dan's right outside the door. He'll get me out.

Before I let my panic get the best of me, I make myself focus on the issue at hand—whatever ghost or creature is in here with me and trying to stay out of harm's way until the crypt doors are opened.

"Hello?" The words are barely a whisper as they leave me, and I try again, attempting to sound braver than I actually am right now. In the dark, alone with...*something*. "Hello?"

Silence.

Great. It wants to play with its prey. Well, I can play too. Anger helps to chase away the panic, and I embrace it like an old friend. Anger has saved my butt on more than one occasion.

"Look, buster, I am not in the mood to play. I have no qualms about opening the Between and tossing you in!"

A chuckle echoes behind me, and I turn, expecting the creepy yellow-eyed kid, but he's not there. Only a vague outline of some kind of square, with another one above it. Fudgepops. It has to be a coffin box thingy. I've seen them in movies, but never expected to see one in real life. What if a zombie pops out, all hungry for brains? Dang it, I have no weapons for zombies. Had Reaper Boy meant zombies? Crap, crap, crapola!

The gentle tap on my shoulder sends me scurrying backward, a scream escaping.

"Easy, it's just me."

Reaper Boy.

"Don't sneak up on me in the dark!" Fury laces my words, but I can't help it.

"I can leave if you want me to." He sounds just as angry as I do.

"No, no, no. Sorry, I'm just freaked out." And as long as he's here, I'm not alone.

"You and me both." A small light appears, casting shadows everywhere, but I can see. It's not bright enough to blind me, but bright enough to make out where we are. The light sits in his hand, like a glowing baseball or something. That's handy.

"Where is it?" He holds out his hand and spins in a circle, and we both scour the area. I see nothing but the crypt box thingy in the middle and two doors, on each side of us, as well as the main door.

"I don't know."

The giggle has him inching closer to me. "What was that?"

I roll my eyes. I hope all reapers aren't as cowardly as he is.

Where is the little bugger? They can hide from even me when they want to.

"What is that?" His voice wavers and he points to the right.

In the corner, a little boy sits hunched over. He's picking at the wounds on his feet. Big holes have been bored into the soles of his feet. Black pus oozes from the blackened wounds, spreading across the paleness of his skin. His hands are mangled. Two of the fingers on his right hand are bent at odd angles, while the thumb on his left hand is gone. What I can see of the left side of his face is caved in, and a large portion of the skin missing. His upper teeth and gum line are clearly visible, and his Adventure Time t-shirt is covered in black stains. Blood. Most people don't realize blood dries in tones of black and browns.

None of that is what horrifies either of us. Usually, a soul has a bright light about it. Even the ones that have gone all demented retain some of that light. This little one's is gone. There is no light about him at all. What's wrong with him?

I take a couple steps toward him, and his head turns, his movement stiff, zombieish. His eyes are glowing with a yellow haze. Not like the other two kids I'd seen. It's like he's being turned or something. His eyes gradually taking on the yellow hue, until there's nothing of him left.

"What's wrong with him?" Reaper Boy's voice is loud in the stillness of the tomb. Those yellow eyes swing to him, and he takes an involuntary step back.

"I was hoping you could tell me."

"I've never seen something like this." The kid hisses at him, and he cringes. "Why is it looking at me like that?"

"He's hungry."

"Hungry?"

He's being turned into one of those creepy kids in my dream that fed upon the soul of the other kid. Reaper Boy is practically glowing with the souls of the people he's reaped today.

"Stay back, or you're going to be his next meal." I take a few more steps toward the kid, making sure to stand in front of the reaper I now find myself having to protect.

When I'm a few feet from him, I stop and squat, praying he doesn't take a bite out of me. I'm made up of ghost energy too. For all I know, I have the same essence inside that the reaper does, which puts me squarely on today's lunch menu. "Hi. I'm Mattie."

He cocks his head, his eyes so full of pain and rage, it makes me ache for him. The reaper in me wants to ease his pain any way I can, but everything else is screaming to run.

"What's your name?" I try again.

He moves faster than I can blink. His hands land on my head, and horrific images flash in front of me. Him. In a room. Horrible pain. Every second of his torture is funneled through me, and I start screaming, unable to stop. A man in a cloak, leaning over him and inhaling deeply while another man tortures him. Laughter. More pain. My entire body shakes with the awful pain. More than that, it's his soul that suffered the worst pain. He felt it. I feel it.

Pain jackknifes through my head, blinding me. An overload of images floods my vision, overwhelming my brain in a way it hasn't been before. It takes its only recourse and shuts down. My vision blurs, and then nothing but blessed silence.

***

~Dan~

I'd seen the crypt door swing open, but she'd been pulled in before I could shout a warning. The door won't budge. Why won't it open? What is in there with her? I don't hear anything. I bang on the door and shout her name, but the only answer I get is silence. Can she hear me through the heavy stone door?

Her panic, her fear, all of it is turning

every nerve cell I have into a living, breathing thing. Her terror pulses in the rapid beating of my own heart. She needs me. I know how she feels about being trapped. I was the one to hold her after every nightmare, assure her she was safe and no one could get to her. No one knows how bad it really was, not even Mary. She hid her fear from everyone. Everyone but me. I'm pretty sure she still has a mild case of PTSD from her time with Mrs. Olson, and being kidnapped by Paul had to have aggravated it. She's spiraling out of control. I feel it eating away at her. My own panic starts to rise. I have to get in there. I pound on the door again. "Mattie!"

My cell phone lights up, and I yank it out. Eli. He must feel her too.

"What's wrong?" My brother doesn't even give me time to say hello.

"Something pulled her into a crypt, and I can't get the door open." I throw the phone down and try once more to pull the door open.

"She's terrified." Frustration and fear coat Eli's voice.

"I know. I feel it too." I have to shout a little because the phone is on the ground.

"You do? You shouldn't be able to. Only her Guardian Angel can do that."

"You're not the only one with a strong bond to her." The words come out with more bite than I intended.

"Young man?"

I turn my head to see the minister who had presided over Meg's funeral frowning at me. "I'm sorry…"

"Reverend Mike. Just call me Reverend Mike. Is something wrong?"

"Yeah, my friend is in here, and now the door won't open."

"How did she get in there?" He frowns and pulls at the door himself. "This one has been closed up for over fifty years, when the last of the family died. No one's opened it since, and Mother Nature took over, sealing it closed with the elements. Are you sure she's in here?"

"Yes, I saw her go in myself." I hesitate a moment, but then blurt out, "I think someone's in there with her. She was dragged inside."

Alarm spreads over the reverend's

face. "Let's get this door open."

"Something dragged her in?" Eli's voice is muffled by the sound of the reverend and me pulling against the door with all our might.

"Dan? What are you doing, and where is Mattie?"

"She's in here, Dad. Somebody dragged her in. We're trying to get the door open, but it's stuck."

"Dragged her in?" He runs up the steps and pushes the reverend aside. The man is older and doesn't need to be doing this. It might give him a heart attack at his age.

Pain lances through my head, and I fall to my knees, clutching my head. Something bad just happened to her. I can feel it.

"Dan?" Dad's voice is panicked, but all I can focus on is this intense pain running rampant everywhere.

"What's wrong? What's going on?" Eli's muffled voice floats up to us.

"Eli?" Dad asks, confused.

"I believe the boy's on the phone." That from the reverend.

Dad picks up my phone. "Eli? Yes, this Dan's father. Something's wrong with him. He's in a lot of pain, and he won't answer me." He listens for a moment. "Mattie? No, she's still inside." Another pause. "Why would getting her out help Dan?" This time I can see his face, and he looks more than a little skeptical.

"Dad." My voice is weak. I'm fading, dark spots dancing in front of my eyes. "He's right. Get her out." I can't black out. Not when she needs me. I blink and force myself to stand. "We have to get her out."

A gasp sounds from behind us, and the reverend is staring at me in a sort of awe. "You have been touched by God, son."

What nonsense is he going on about? Even Dad looks at him like he's nuts. Then again, my parents aren't religious. Neither am I, not really, but Mattie is.

Reverend Mike lays a hand upon my arm, and it burns where he touches me. I try to yank my arm away, but he holds on like a dog with a bone. "You hold one of the sacred swords."

How does he know that?

"I saw it when you stood up." He nods to my back.

That's not true. I gave the sword to Caleb and Eli for safekeeping.

"Not the actual sword." The reverend laughs when I glare at him. "It's more of an outline of white light. I see it because I held one myself once. You can open the door, son. You just have to draw strength from the sword and ask for help."

"Dan, what is he talking about?" Dad holds me as I sway, fighting to keep from blacking out. "You do not own a sword."

Another white-hot bolt of pain nearly buckles my knees. The darkness leaches away more of my vision. At this point, I'm willing to try anything. Eli has to be going through the same thing. I need to help all three of us.

I stagger over to the door, pushing my dad aside, and lay my hands on the heavy iron rings that serve as a door handle for the crypt. I pull, and it doesn't give.

"No, son." The reverend is right behind me. "Think about the sword, think about how strong it makes you feel when you hold it. Focus on that and pray. Pray for help, and when you feel all that strength build up, then pull."

Doing as he says, I close my eyes and think about the sword. The image appears instantly. I don't even have to work to conjure it up. It had been heavy in my hands the night the angel handed it to me. I'd felt more than just the physical weight of the sword. I'd felt the responsibility of possessing it, the responsibility of using it to help those around me who had no other recourse. I'd felt the weight of truth. The sword and I merged that night. It became a part of me. I'd not thought about it because I didn't want to remember, but now I have to face the truth. My truth. It's a warrior's sword, a holy warrior. Whether I want to admit God's real or not, I can't hide from the truth. The sword makes us face truth.

Dear God, help me. Help me open this door.

The prayer is simple, a hesitant utterance, but the result is immediate.

Strength surges through my being, and the blackness eating away at my vision gives way to a blinding bluish white light, and I pull, I pull with all my might, and the door swings outward, nearly knocking us to our feet.

And then I see her, lying unconscious on the floor, with that thing bent over her, its hands on her head. Without thought, I rush forward and reach to grab it, but someone pulls me back. I turn, ready to smite whatever else is in here, and stop mid-strike.

The reaper.

The one who'd come to collect me. I remember him. He looks terrified, but resolute.

"We can't hurt it."

"Of course we can. It's hurting her."

"No." The reaper shakes his head. "I saw what it showed her. It's a lost soul, trying to escape the monster who is consuming it. It came to her, her ghost light a beacon to it. It wants help. We can't hurt it."

"But it's hurting her!" When the next wave of pain hits, I do fall. "It's hurting all of us."

"Why did no one tell me this?" Anger burns in the reaper's eyes. "I was not told your soul was connected to hers. This changes everything."

The reverend squats beside me while Dad rushes over to Mattie. He's lightly tapping her cheeks to try to wake her up, but he can't. I've seen this. The night the first ghost attacked her at Zeke's. We'd pulled her away from it before it could inflict any real harm, before I'd felt any of the pain.

"Who are you talking to, son?"

"Dad." My voice is low, almost strangled. "Pull her outside. Hurry." The reverend helps me to my feet then guides me outside. The moment Dad picks Mattie up, the pain stops. Instantly. No more pain.

The last thing I see is the pissed off face of a reaper before my eyes fall shut, my mind finally succumbing to the darkness of blessed oblivion.

Chapter Three

~*Mattie*~

My head is flipping killing me. That's the first thought I have upon waking up in the hospital. I touch it gingerly, trying to remember what caused me to end up here yet again. The beeping of the machines is a telltale sign I'm in the hospital. I don't even have to open my eyes to confirm it.

"I know you're awake."

Eli. "Turn the lights down if you want me to open my eyes. I have a headache the size of Mount Everest."

There is a bit of rustling, and I sense him standing next to me, reaching above me to dim the lights. "You're good to go,

Hilda."

I hate the cursed nickname he gave me. He shortened my name, Mathilda, down to Hilda. Irritates me to no end.

"Don't call me that."

"There she is." He leans down and places a soft kiss across my lips, and that familiar warm, tingly sensation starts. "You scared me, Hilda."

"What happened?" I don't remember anything past speaking to Meg's dad at the funeral. After that, it's a big empty space.

"You don't remember?" Confusion stamps his expression. "A ghost attacked you at the cemetery."

Nope, not ringing any bells. Just a big old black hole of nothing. This is the second time a ghost attacked me and I can't remember it.

"Where's Dan?" He's usually here when I wake up in the hospital.

"Talking to your dad, I think." There's something in his voice that causes me to look up at him. Jealousy flickers in those beautiful aqua orbs. Before I can question him, Mary's mom bustles in. She's in her uniform, so I'm betting she's my nurse for the night. Technically, Zeke has custody of me, so they can't not let her be my nurse anymore. As my foster mother, she couldn't have cared for me. Family can't take care of family, but that's moot now.

"Visiting hours are over, Eli." The no-nonsense mom tone has him backing away, hands up. "You can come back tomorrow."

He purses his lips, but doesn't argue. "I'll be back first thing in the morning." He leans down and kisses me. It's a kiss that says a lot, a lot more than he could say. He's jealous and trying to prove I belong to him in that kiss. It leaves me breathless and staring after him when he walks away.

"If a man kissed me like that, I wouldn't be staring after him looking perplexed." Mrs. Cross fusses with the blankets before taking my blood pressure.

"Dan kissed me." Why did I blurt that out? I close my eyes and groan.

"Well, that explains the perplexed look." Mrs. Cross laughs as she waits for the blood pressure pump.

"Why does it explain it?"

"Because you're confused." She pauses while she waits for my numbers. "Anyone who isn't blind knows how Dan feels about you, and you him."

"But he wasn't interested...I mean, he was dating Meg."

"You like Eli, don't you?" She sits on the bed. "You can have feelings for other people, especially when you push your real feelings to the side. Dan saw you as being too young for him, and I never expected the thing with Meg to last."

"Why not?"

"Because he loves you. When someone loves someone the way he loves you, no one will ever compare. That has a way of causing problems in a relationship."

"So you think Eli and I will turn out the same way because I have feelings for Dan?"

She shrugs. "I don't know, Mattie. What you have with Eli is new and could be just as powerful. Who knows what might happen? You have to figure out how you feel about them both."

"That doesn't really help, you know," I grouch. "It just makes it more confusing."

"Moms are notorious for making things more confusing." Mrs. Cross smiles. "We do the best we can and give you the best advice we have. It's up to you to figure out what pearls of wisdom to garner from our confusing diatribe."

"Thanks, Mrs. Cross." Not that she'd helped me, but she tried, and that's what counts.

"Mattie, no one can ever replace your mom, but I *am* a mom, and I'm always here for you whenever you need me. I hope you know that."

Now I feel bad about grouching at her. She's the best foster mom ever. "I know that, Mrs. Cross. Thank you."

She squeezes my hand then stands, but I stop her before she can leave.

"Is there a reason I'm here other than passing out?" I'm hooked up to a ton of machines, the one connected to electrodes on my head the most concerning.

The frown in her eyes worries me.

"We're still waiting on some tests to come back, but once we have all the information, I will come talk to you."

I nod, not feeling very confident. There's something she's not telling me. Something that has her worried, maybe even scared. Don't tell me after all this time, they found a brain tumor or something.

When she leaves, I can't shake the feeling something's wrong. Maybe it's because I can't remember anything. Could a brain tumor cause me to black out like that with no memory? It can't be a brain tumor, though. They would have seen that the last time they ran a CT, which wasn't that long ago.

I'm probably stressing over nothing. Anemia, maybe. I mean, I'm always so cold, maybe they are concerned about me having low blood or something.

"Why do you look freaked out?"

A calmness washes over my emotions at the sound of Dan's voice. It's not the same type of calm Eli inspires. Eli literally takes all my worry away like magic. At least until he leaves, and then it's back full force. Dan has the ability to settle my nerves, and I stay that way. Even after he leaves. Simply because he's Dan. Is it friendship or something else? I just don't know! Why do boys have to be so confusing?

"Because I *am* freaked out, and you weren't here when I woke up." I can't hold back the accusation. He's always here. I count on that.

"Yeah, sorry, I just spent the last hour answering questions from your father and Mr. Malone…James." He says it like he can't quite bring himself to call his birth father by his given name. He can't call him Dad, though. He has a dad, a really good one. I understand how weird this is for him. Heck, I can't bring myself to say *Dad* either when I speak to my own father. We've known each other about the same amount of time Dan has known about the Malones. It's weird.

"Questions?"

"Yeah, about the ghost at the cemetery."

"Ghost?" What ghost is he talking about? The Confederate soldier? He seemed so nice, though. Not a spark of malice in him. I'd planned on offering to help him cross over if he'd wanted me to.

His brown eyes darken. "You don't remember?"

"The last thing I remember is talking to Mr. Johnson." When his lips thin out, I know something is really wrong. "What's going on, Dan? Mrs. Cross is worried, and I can see you are too. What's wrong with me?"

"You had a seizure, Mattie." He runs a hand through his hair. "A big one. They saw it on your CT scan."

Seizure? That can't be at all good. "That's a bad thing, right?"

"Yes, it's very bad." He falls into the chair beside the bed. "If you keep having them, they can lead to complications. Serious complications like stroke, brain damage…death."

Now I understand why Mrs. Cross didn't want to tell me anything until she knew all the facts. She wasn't just worried. She was scared. But so am I. Death is no joke.

"Do they know what caused it?"

"No, *ma petite*, they do not." Zeke answers my question from where he's hovering in the doorway. "But I have a theory."

When he comes in and I can see him clearly, I'm shocked. He looks haggard, worry lines around his eyes. His clothes are wrinkled, like he's slept in them or something. "How long have I been out?"

"Since we found you unconscious yesterday." Dan rubs his eyes wearily. I hadn't thought anything about him wearing the same clothes. I assumed it was still today—well, yesterday now.

Dan looks even more tired than Zeke, if that's possible. It reminds me of the night I woke up after he found me at the old group home where Mrs. Olson held me and Mary. That's when I started to realize it wasn't so bad letting someone care about me. The sheer relief on his face when he saw me wake up told me maybe I was worth someone's love. He'd looked worn out then, and that's what he looks like now.

"The ghost that attacked you…"

"She doesn't remember anything," Dan

interrupts him.

"What?" Zeke turns his blue eyes on me. "You remember nothing, *ma petite*?"

"Not a thing." I shake my head and wince. Not a good idea. My head is truly killing me.

"This is the second time this has happened." A darkness fills Zeke's eyes. "I do not think that is a coincidence."

"I'm not following." Why do people always try to make you think when your head is the size of a watermelon with someone shooting it full of BBs? So not cool. I look up and see Reaper Boy behind them. He puts a finger to his lips and shakes his head. Why doesn't he want anyone to know he's here?

"These ghosts are malicious, Mattie. Someone is sending them to you, someone who means to harm you." Zeke's eyes glow with suppressed rage. This is the man everyone warned me about, the man who is a criminal, the man who doesn't hesitate when it comes to what he wants, no matter what he has to do. It should scare me, but it doesn't. He's angry *for* me and not *at* me. Maybe that's the difference.

"You think the ghost caused the seizure?" I squint, my eyes finally starting to hurt against the light, soft though it may be.

"I'm sure of it." Zeke starts to pace. "Both times these ghosts attacked, you've lost consciousness and your memory. I don't believe in coincidences, Emma Rose."

Zeke sometimes slips up and uses the birth name he'd given me, Emma Rose Crane. I've been Mattie Hathaway for so long, he agreed to let me keep my name. Doesn't mean it's easy for him to call me that, especially when he's upset. The only other person to call me Emma Rose is Silas, my demonic grandfather.

Reaper Boy shakes his head at me again. Does he mean don't say anything or that Zeke is wrong? I do not speak Mime.

"Ghosts find me all the time." I sit up a little more, searching for water. My mouth is dry. Dan stands and pours it without me having to ask him. We've done this dance several times before. I wake up after days unconscious, and he hands me water. "They probably just wanted my help."

"No, Mattie. This ghost, it was different." Dan hands me the little plastic cup then sits back down. "I could see it, which means it had already flipped its evil switch. This thing, I don't know how to describe it. It was intent upon…feeding off you. That's the best analogy I can come up with. It was bent over you, and I could see your energy flowing into it. Think Harry Potter and the Dementors."

"It *fed* off me?" A freaking ghost fed off me? No, no, no…we are figuring this thing out. Nothing gets to munch on me. Nope, not happening. Then reality decides to laugh at me by reminding me I black out when these particular ghosts come knocking. Can't defend myself unconscious. Dang it!

"What kind of ghosts can feed like that?" Dan rolls his head, stretching his neck.

"I do not know." Zeke's Creole accents thickens with his anger.

There's a knock, and my old social worker, Nancy Moriarity, walks in, all brisk and businesslike. She heads straight for me, wrapping me in a hug. I owe everything to this woman. No matter how terrible I got, she never gave up on me.

"Are you okay? What happened?" She doesn't give me even a second to nod before whirling on my father, her finger stabbing him in the chest. "You! You have her for less than a week and she's back in the hospital! What did you do?"

Zeke's eyebrows race to his hairline, and he backs up with each tap of her finger against his chest. He looks alarmed. No one's ever handled Zeke, except my social worker. Nancy rocks.

"I did nothing, *madame*. She attended her friend's funeral and had a seizure."

"Seizure?" She pales and takes a shaky breath. "What's wrong with her?"

"They do not know." Zeke slides away from her, his expression a mix between anger, admiration, and irritation. "I assure you, I've already contacted the best neurosurgeon in the country. He's on a plane as we speak."

Whoa! Neurosurgeon? Surely one seizure doesn't warrant flying in some fancy doctor?

"Calm down, Mattie." Nancy shoots a glare at Zeke. "Your father's precautionary measures don't mean you're at death's door."

She knows me so well.

"Of course, she's not at death's door. She's a Crane. Death would flee before her."

Grandparents. I'd forgotten all about them, but there they are, walking into the room all concerned and grandparenty. Six months ago, I'd have been over the moon. Right now, I just want everyone to go away so I can think and figure out this ghost thing. I've done it by myself for so long, it's hard to let anyone else in except for Dan. He's...well, he's Dan.

"My darling, are you well?" Lila Crane, who doesn't look old enough to be my grandmother, bends down and kisses me on the forehead. "You look pale. Why are the lights so dim?"

"They're dim because she has a massive headache and the light makes it worse." Dan speaks up as Lila reaches for the dimmer switch.

"Oh...of course, *ma petite chou*. I should have realized." She's very formal, and can be intimidating. She'd tried that on me once, but I don't intimidate. She turns those deep blue eyes on Nancy, her expression becoming cold. "And you are?"

"Nancy Moriarity, Mattie's social worker." Nancy's back stiffens and her expression turns professional.

"Ah, but she is no longer in foster care, is she? Or were we misinformed?" Haughty. Yup, Lila sounds haughty, which isn't sitting well with Nancy. Not one bit.

"The hospital called me. I'm still listed as her social worker in their files. Whether she's still under my direct care or not, her welfare will *always* be my concern. I dare anyone to say otherwise."

Point for Nancy, I think?

"We appreciate your concern, Ms. Moriarity." My grandfather attempts to diffuse a potential situation. "Our girl means the world to us, and anyone looking out for her has our deepest respect. Isn't that right, Lila?"

Lila gives Nancy a tight smile. "Of course."

"What I think Mattie needs more than anything right now is rest." Dan stands and faces them. "Some peace and quiet until her headache calms down a bit."

Lila directs frosty eyes at Dan, and his expression changes to that famous cop face—bland, bored, and emotionless. I've come to learn that's when he's most invested. I've tried to mimic that expression, and it always ends up in an epic fail. So not fair. They must teach it to them at the police academy. Dan denies it, but I'm guaranteeing it's a trade secret.

"Daniel is right, Mama." Zeke intervenes before Lila can say anything else. "She's in pain, and the best thing for her is rest."

Lila purses her lips. "Ezekiel, we've only just found her, and she's hurt. She needs to know her family is here and…"

"But I do know." I blink against the blinding pain thumping behind my eyes. I know where Lila's overprotectiveness is coming from. "I know you're here, and I know you love me. My head just really hurts right now, and I need some quiet."

"I doubt you will get your grandmamma to go farther than the waiting room." Zeke walks over to me, reaches down and pushes a stray strand of hair behind my ear. "We were all frightened, *ma petite*. We *did* only just find you after years of not knowing. The thought of leaving you here alone…" He shakes his head, and I see the fear in his eyes.

Another crack of pain makes me gasp and grab my head. What is going on? I've never had a headache like this. The pain is intense.

"What is it?" Dan's voice seems to come from far away. "Mattie? What's wrong? Get a nurse!"

My world melts away, and the only thing I feel is a rolling, pulsing agony in my head. What is wrong with me?

My vision blurs, and the world tilts, and I hear a lot of shouting.

Then it all goes black.

Chapter Four

The next time I open my eyes, the room is dark, the only light from a gap in the bathroom door. A quick look around confirms Zeke passed out in one chair and Dan in the other. Dan's pulled his chair closer, his head resting on the mattress. At least they're sleeping.

My head is pounding. What happened?

"You had another seizure."

Reaper Boy stands at the foot of my bed, arms crossed, looking all pissed off. Why is he mad? Did I do something I don't remember? He's still wearing that same t-shirt and jeans I always see him in.

Another seizure? Not good.

"No, it's not good," he agrees.

Wait…can he hear what I'm thinking?

He cracks a small smile. "Yes, Mattie, I can hear what you're thinking. I'm your guide, so I hear you. How else would I know if you needed me?"

"Do you have a name?" I can't keep calling him Reaper Boy if he's going to be invading my privacy on a regular basis.

"Reaper Boy?" He shakes his head. "My name is Kane, with a K."

Like Abel and Cain?

"Nope, no relation."

Dan stirs and we both glance at him. When he settles back down, I turn my attention to Kane. "Do you know why I'm having seizures? I wasn't sure earlier if you were shaking your head no to Zeke's idea of someone trying to hurt me, or just no in general."

A heavy sigh escapes him. "Mattie, your abilities are waking up, so to speak, only they shouldn't be. You're gaining the abilities of a full reaper, and your body is still very much a human shell. It's not built to withstand what a full-fledged reaper can."

"So?" I prompt when he goes silent.

"So, your brain can't handle the overload, and it's seizing."

Nope, so not good.

"Every time a ghost comes to you, every time one touches you to show you what they're trying to say and can't, your reaping abilities rush up and try to sort it out. Only your brain, it's not equipped to do that. It strains it so much that you seize. I'm not sure what to do to help you. I must go talk with the council and see if there is anything we can do to stop this from harming you."

"And if there isn't anything they can do?" I know I shouldn't be asking questions I sort of already know the answer to, but I *need* to know.

"Then you'll die."

Fudgepops.

"There is something else I need to speak with you about." He looks more worried than when he told me I might die. What could be worse than my potential death?

"You don't remember anything from the cemetery?"

I shake my head.

"The spirit of a child came to you. Its soul was so damaged, there was almost nothing left of it. Just a spark. I couldn't see it, but you could, even if you didn't realize it. It wanted help, and your light shines brighter than my own. I saw that tiny light left inside it through your reaping energy. When you offered help, it latched onto you, showing you what had happened to it, trying to escape its pain and move on before it was consumed."

"Then the overload hit?"

"Yes, you blacked out before you could help the little one. Rage replaced hope in the spirit, and what was left of its soul died, and it changed…it became something that we've feared for a long time."

What could possibly scare a reaper?

"Do you remember when we talked about the Fallen One, Deleriel?"

I nod, my mind already three steps ahead of him.

"He feeds off the broken souls of children, those souls enduring an eternity of suffering where it resides. Before, the souls were never able to roam freely amongst humans."

"That's changed." My dream of the yellow-eyed boy as well as the little boy in the morgue flash like warning bells.

"It has, but that's not the worrisome part. Souls have never been able to break away from Deleriel, but now they are. That's because of *you*, Mattie. Your light shines so brightly, it calls to them, gives them the strength and courage to flee. Straight to you."

I can't help that. Why is he looking at me like it's my fault?

"Deleriel chooses certain souls to join his army of child soldiers. You've seen them? The yellow-eyed demonic children?"

"Yeah." Scary little buggers.

"The two souls that have escaped him and fled to you…they became something more than a vengeful spirit. Deleriel never lets his souls die. He needs them to feed him while he's trapped in the underworld, even his children. They *all* feed him. The two that beelined to your light…when their hope died, what was left of their souls died. There is nothing left in them, no hope, no joy, no pain, no fear. The perfect storm to create a monster."

"So they're out there killing people now?"

"They are devouring innocent ghosts, those wandering around lost, confused, and afraid. Once they gain enough strength, they'll go after the living. The soul of a living person is ten times brighter than a ghost. Because of the life force that powers it. Good or bad, a person's soul is the brightest and most powerful energy source on the planet. Once the rogue children have gained enough power, they'll be unstoppable. We're afraid that if Deleriel realizes the type of power source they are, he'll get what he always wanted."

"Which is?"

"To escape hell forever. He hates it there. Before he fell, he looked after the souls of children. He protected them, especially the ones who suffered at the hands of those charged to care for them. When he fell, his desire to protect didn't change. It did morph into something twisted, but it's why he surrounds himself with children now. He protects the child army he's created, cares for them the way any father would for their children. He even loves them in a depraved sort of way."

"You make it sound like he's a good guy at heart." But that makes no sense. Aren't fallen angels bad things?

"Fallen or not, he's an angel, Mattie. Good exists inside of him, only it's warped and twisted. He may protect his children from outside forces, but he still feeds off them, still causes them pain so they will be what his black soul needs to survive."

And that thing wants Mary? No way, no how is he getting his hands on her.

"We're veering off topic and my time is limited." He shifts, and his eyes seem to lose focus for a minute, like he's seeing something I can't. When he blinks, there is an urgency in them that wasn't there before. "Deleriel seeks permanent entry into this world. If he finds these two before we do, he'll realize they can provide him with the energy he needs to stay above ground. Not only that, but he'll let more souls die and send them out."

"So he'll get the juice he needs by collecting those supercharged ghosties after they've pigged out?" I frown, thinking. "But if he feeds off souls, and the souls of those kids die, how does that help him? He can't feed off them anymore if they don't possess a soul, can he?"

"A soul is made up of pure energy. Those children are feeding off energy, the same as Deleriel. All he has to do is consume that energy when it's released."

"He'd kill them to release the energy?" And boom, Deleriel would never have to go back to the underworld. He could just keep feeding on the soulless chock full of the energy they've consumed.

"Exactly."

"Freaking great," I mutter. Now I have to worry about this, on top of everything else.

"We need to find the person who is helping Deleriel," Kane continues. "He can't take a corporeal form here on Earth without great difficulty, so he usually acts through a human vessel. Find the vessel, find the missing girl. I believe the last child tried to show you where they were, but your memories of it are either gone or buried. If you can eliminate the vessel, you can send Deleriel back to his own hell."

"Can't he just pop into another vessel?" Angels do it all the time on *Supernatural*. It's one of the few paranormal shows I enjoy. Then again, it could just be Dean I enjoy.

"Real life isn't like TV, Mattie. There aren't multiple vessels for angels to play musical chairs with. This vessel is one Deleriel has cultivated since the time of its birth. He's made the man as twisted as he is so it can hold his true essence. As evil as mankind can be, it takes someone truly evil to hold the Devourer of Children."

The Devourer of Children. Just the name makes me shiver. "How am I supposed to help if I keep blacking out when they get near me?"

"Not when they get near you. It's only when they touch you." He blinks and rubs his eyes. Can reapers get tired? "We have to figure out how to keep you alive long enough to help. Your brain is damaged, and if you keep seizing, it won't last much longer. It would be easier if you died and became a reaper, but for some reason, those in charge do not want that."

"Dying's not an option, Kane. If I die, Dan dies."

"Something I just discovered yesterday." The bite in his voice isn't directed at me. At least I hope not. "It changes many things, including the need to keep you alive. I must go, but, Mattie, remember what I told you in the Between and try not to do anything stupid until I return."

And just like that, he's gone. There one second, and then *poof*, gone the next. Now that is a cool reaping ability I wouldn't mind having.

I'd fled to the Between in the morgue to escape what I now believe was Deleriel and the last victim before Kayla.

It takes three days for the soul to leave the body. He was there to collect. Kane showed up to help me navigate safely through the white zone that is the Between with the little ghost girl I'd saved from them.

While there, he'd told me I had to worry about the people in charge upstairs. They're afraid of me, apparently. I don't think he meant God. I think he means other players within that realm—his reaping supervisors, maybe? I just don't know. Either way, he said as soon as I take care of Deleriel, they would take care of me. It hadn't really inspired any urgency to deal with said demon. Unfortunately, this whole remaining on Earth thing has caused me to rethink it. I can't sit by and do nothing. If he's allowed to stay here, the havoc he could rain down upon us all? Not good.

I'm not sure what I can do right now, though. My brain is not cooperating. Just talking to Kane for as long as I did made my headache worse. Sleep is probably the best thing for me. I can figure all this out in the morning.

Chapter Five

The humming is nice. It reminds me of an old lullaby my mom sang to me when I was little. I can't remember the words, but I remember the sound of her voice and the rhythm of the song. It's soothing.

When I open my eyes, my calm turns to alarm. I'm in a bedroom, only it's not mine. The walls are a blood red, the floor black tile. The humming is coming from somewhere beyond the open doorway. Where the heck am I?

Should I go investigate? I mean, that's how the stupid person in the horror movie dies. They go and investigate. But I can't stay here, can I? If I'm in some weird memory thingy, I have to go see what's up. It has to be either a memory or my own dark and twisty dream. Either way, sitting here in a bed isn't going to change things.

I hop down, noticing I'm in my favorite penguin pajamas. At least that's one plus. Dream me is going for comfort. The hard tile beneath my feet is freezing cold, and I wince with every step I take. No slippers anywhere to be found. When I reach the doorway, I pause. The hall before me is empty, barely lit with some recessed lighting turned low.

Listening to the sounds of the lullaby, I start walking down the hallway. This place is creepy with its dark flooring and even darker walls. Where am I? I've never been here before, at least not that I can remember. When I round the corner, I stop, staring at the scene before me.

There's a table with a body on it, and the white sheet draped over it sets off alarm bells. An easel is set up next to the table, the blank canvas waiting for the artist to begin. Old mason jars, the kind you use for canning foods, sit on a smaller table, along with several brushes. The dark brick behind the easel pulses a bit, the wall itself alive with something.

I *have* been here before. Only once, though, and that was enough. I turn to run, but I can't. I'm frozen. I look down and see my feet encased in ice. It creeps up my legs, and I can't move. No, no, no! Not again. I struggle, but it's useless, and I know it. I'm not getting out of this until he decides to let me.

The painter enters the room, humming the lullaby that had soothed me before. It's gone past that to blatant, all-consuming fear.

Silas.

What does he want? Memories of our last meeting intrude. He'd flayed a strip of skin from my face, and then healed it. He'd promised me more pain if I didn't start doing what he wanted—learning to bring my drawings to life with my own blood.

"Good morning, my darling girl."

His British accent is quite pronounced today. Usually, it's not so thick. He's either very happy or extremely upset. You can never tell with him.

"What do you want?" I keep my voice

calm, or as calm as I can. Grandfather or not, Silas terrifies me.

"No 'good morning, Grandpapa'?" Silas walks over to the table and pulls the sheet back. A man lies there, his blue eyes fixed on Silas. He's about forty or so, the few streaks of white in his chestnut hair attesting to his age. It's his expression you can't look away from, though, it's one of abject fear. Silas picks up one of the mason jars, inspecting it. A small whimper escapes the man on the table.

"Good morning, Silas." I force the words out. He's being civil, but that could change in a heartbeat. His moods flip-flop so often. I have no desire to set him off into a rage. I can't move, so I can't protect myself from his wrath.

"Emma Rose, meet Cordell Reyes." Silas puts the jar down and picks up another. "He made a deal with me ten years ago, and he didn't want to honor our deal when his contract came due."

The man on the table makes a sound between a strangled sob and a cry of pain. His eyes are wide, the whites more prominent than even the blue of the irises. I look around, trying to find something to help him with, but immobile as I am, there's nothing I can do. I'm angry because Silas has put me in this situation where I have to watch whatever he's going to do.

"You pity him?" Silas turns to face me. "Would you still pity Cordell if I told you he sold his soul to gain access to his parents' fortune so he could spend it on his own perverse peculiarities?"

The man in question closes his eyes, shame written all over his face. He'd killed his parents so he could…I shake my head, unable to even think about what he might have wanted to do.

"I arranged for their deaths while he was out of the country. He's spent the last ten years indulging in his fantasies as promised. Now, it's time to pay the piper. Deals must be honored. Remember that, Emma Rose. If you make a deal, it must always be honored. Our word is our bond."

"I'm not making any deals, Silas."

"But you will, my darling girl, you

will." Silas turns and picks up the man's arm, his fingernails tracing the soft flesh of the underside. "Do you remember your first lesson? What I told you about the blood?"

The first time I had met Silas was in a dream, in this very studio. He'd shown me a painting of a woman. The same woman who'd occupied his metal table beside the canvas. Her soul had been trapped in the painting utilizing her blood. The soul resides in the blood, constantly flowing, growing, changing. He'd used *my* blood to finish the painting, and it had breathed life into it. The woman seemed to move, her emotions a living, breathing thing right there on the canvas. My blood did that.

"I remember."

"Wonderful." He pierces the man's arm with a razor-sharp nail then lowers it so it hangs off the table. He sets the large mason jar beneath his hand, and the blood slowly trickles down his arm, winding around his hands and falling drop by drop into the jar.

"Where are my manners?" Silas whirls

around. "I am not used to company, so you'll have to forgive me. Would you like breakfast, child? I can whip up something, whatever you like."

"No, I'm not hungry." My stomach churns at the thought of eating while Silas drains the man's blood to use for paint.

"It's just as well. We have much to accomplish while they are busy trying to save you."

"What do you mean trying to save me?" Alarm flares up. What's he talking about?

"You are having a major seizure, my darling girl." He says it matter-of-factly, prepping his brushes. "I called your soul here while they are working on you."

"Why?" I can't keep the suspicion out of my voice. Silas never does anything without an agenda.

"Why? To keep you safe, of course." He checks the mason jar and *tsks*. It's not filling up fast enough for him. He stands and runs a fingernail across the man's chest. Blood wells up, and Silas dips his brush into it. "Don't worry, Emma Rose,

I'm not going to let you die. I have too many plans for you."

Don't worry? Easier said than done. He's standing here telling me my body is going through a major seizure, causing who knows what kind of damage, and he expects me not to worry just on his say so? So not gonna happen.

His brush soaks up the sticky substance and I watch, fascinated, despite my disgust and worry over what's going on outside this dream as Silas begins his first brush strokes across the canvas.

He's very, very good. Each movement is fluid, beautiful. There is joy on his face as he paints. Nancy told me once that the only time she'd ever seen me happy was when I was drawing. She said I'd looked joyous. I wonder if I get that from Silas. It would be just my luck, the one true talent I have would come from a demon.

"Now, Emma Rose, if I free you, can I trust you not to try to escape? I'm in no mood to chase you down. Nor do I want you running into one of my hounds. They can be testy about trespassers."

No, I do not want to be on the wrong

end of one of his hellhounds. I watch *Supernatural.* If Silas's beasts are even a tenth as nasty as Crowley's, I want no part of them.

"I won't run."

And just like that, I'm free. The ice is gone from around my feet and legs. I lean down and rub them, relieving some of the ache from the cold. "Thank you."

"You are most welcome. Please, sit." He motions to the chair beside his easel. I hadn't noticed it before. Or perhaps he made it magically appear when he needed it.

I start to refuse, but decide against it. A civil Silas isn't as dangerous as an irritated Silas. I have to admit the chair is more comfortable than it looks. My legs are sore from standing immobile for so long anyway.

"Have you given any thought to our discussion?" Silas goes back to painting, and I notice the man's face is beginning to look more alive, the details transforming an outline into expression and contours.

"About Deleriel?"

He nods, beginning to hum. It *is* the same lullaby my mom used to sing to me. How does Silas know it?

"I'm not sure what you expect me to do. I'm a reaper, Silas. I deal in ghosts, not fallen angels turned demonic. I don't even know where to begin."

"Yes, Emma Rose, you are a reaper, but you aren't *just* a reaper. There are so many layers to you, layers you don't even know about yet. Take your visions, for example. That comes from the shaman gift that runs through your bloodline."

I'd almost forgotten about that. My great-something-or-other grandmother happened to have powerful shamans in her family. It was why Silas chose her to be the mother of his child. It was the beginning of the selective breeding that produced me as the end result. It freaks me out just thinking about it. He'd essentially produced me in a lab, only one of his making instead of a scientific, clinical laboratory.

"You have abilities that you haven't discovered, doors in your mind that still need to be opened. One door in particular." Silas studies the painting as he speaks. "You remember that your birth mother made a pact with Deleriel for a child with certain abilities?"

"Yes." Melissa had basically sold me to save herself. I still haven't even let myself think about that. One mother tried to murder me to protect me, the other to save herself. I sure did win the lottery on motherly affection.

"Your mother came to me, as I told you, and I arranged the circumstances that would produce you. There is only one ability that Deleriel seeks, one ability that cannot be cultivated from the human pool here on this plane of existence."

My skin crawls at the implications in his tone. What does he mean, *this* plane of existence?

"Your mother…"

"She's not my mother." I stop him there. It's the one thing about this whole mess I've come to reconcile myself with. Melissa wanted me dead because it served her selfish needs. That is not what a mother does. Claire did what she did to protect me. *She's* my mother. Always will be. Zeke may always resent that, but it is the truth. Claire Hathaway is and will always be my mother.

Silas turns and regards me curiously. "She is your mother, though. She gave birth to you."

A short, bitter laugh escapes. "Giving birth to someone doesn't qualify you to be a parent. Parents love their kids, protect them as best they can. They would die themselves before letting harm come to their child. Georgina Dupres is not my mother. She just happens to be the woman I share DNA with. Nothing more, nothing less."

"Amanda Sterling tried to kill you, my darling girl, but you think of her as your mother?" True curiosity burned in his eyes.

I forget that Claire's real name is Amanda Sterling, Dan's adoptive mother's sister too. It's odd when I hear people call my mom Amanda. She's been Claire to me since I was old enough to understand her name wasn't just Mama.

"Mom wasn't trying to hurt me, Silas." I shift in my seat, trying to find the words to explain it. "She was protecting me."

"Protecting you by sticking a knife in you eight times? That says rage to me, Emma Rose. Overkill. She could have simply slit your throat, stabbed you in the gut, used poison...but to stab you so many times?" He shakes his head, clearly not in my lane of thinking.

"She was also high on heroin. I doubt she knew how many times she stabbed me." I tell myself that all the time. Silas's words are the same questions I've run through my own mind countless times over the years, though. He could be right, and I could be terribly wrong about her intentions, but I choose to believe my mom was doing her best to protect me.

"She was far from perfect, Silas, but before the drugs consumed her, she was the best mom ever. She loved me, and that's what I hold on to."

He purses his lips. "Had I known she would turn to drugs, I would never have allowed her to take you."

"What?" I glance up sharply. He *allowed* her to take me?

He nods, stroking his chin. "I realized

Georgina was about to offer you up to Deleriel. It was I who convinced her to allow Amanda to whisk you off. I slipped into her mind while she slept and whispered to her. I convinced her in order to keep you safe *for* Deleriel, she had to let you go. It was only after Amanda locked her in that night, that I withdrew from her mind. I thanked her, but I warned her he would be in a rage. I gave her a chance to protect herself, but she chose to face him, thinking she could barter a new deal. Stupid woman. He punished her as I knew he would. She's trapped in her mind, locked in her own personal hell."

My family tree is so twisted, I long for blissful ignorance again.

"Amanda's job was to care for you, to hide you from everyone who might come looking. I visited her several times in those first few months, and it seemed fine, so I left the two of you alone. It wasn't until you were four that I looked in again and discovered her new habits."

"That day, she'd been railing about the painter...she meant you."

"Yes. All she knew was that I was a painter who had helped her. Someone started whispering in her ear, telling her things she didn't need to know. To this day, I do not know who it was. They told her about you, your lineage. She went from trying to protect you from an abusive father to protecting you from supernatural forces. I think that is what drove her to drugs, in all honesty. She couldn't handle the truth. The Sterlings are a ruthless bunch. I never knew she'd be the weakest one."

"She wasn't weak." I stand and face him. "My mom *was not* weak. She couldn't protect me, and she knew it. So she did the only thing she could do. She thought if I were dead, then no one could get to me."

"And how do you know that?"

"Because she killed herself too, Silas. She whispered to me that I'd be safe now, and I lay there and watched the life go out of her eyes. She wasn't crazy, she wasn't evil, she was just my mama, and she did the best she could." I wipe the tears away and take a step closer. "If you call her weak again, I don't care what you can do to me. I *will* hurt you."

The smile that spreads across his face has me stumbling backward. It's not a nice smile. It's the smile I give right before I launch an attack on someone, be it verbal or physical. My body tenses, preparing to fight. I've tipped the demon over the edge.

He stalks over to me, the smile getting creepier by the minute. When his hand comes up to cup my cheek, I can't help the flinch. The last time he'd lain a hand on me had been quite painful.

"You have no idea how much you please me, my darling girl." He takes my hand and leads me over to the painting. "Come, tell me what you think."

This is not what I'm expecting. He's being nice. I peer at him out of the corner of my eye, and yup, that same smile is still there. What's he up to?

Instead of trying to figure it out, I focus on the painting. No sense in trying to guess what a demon is thinking. It'll just drive me mad. The portrait isn't anywhere near done, but even at this stage, something's missing. The lines and the brush strokes are perfect, the image, rough as it is, is still beautiful. But there's something missing.

Silas turns me to face the man lying on the table, whimpering, his eyes wide with fear and a plea for help. "Look at him, Emma Rose. What do you see?"

"A poor, helpless guy?" I can't keep the sarcasm at bay. It was such an obvious question.

"We've already discussed his trespasses, Emma Rose. He's not someone to pity. Look at him, see what's beneath the surface, what's missing from his painting."

How much more cryptic could he be? What am I supposed to be looking for? I turn my attention back to his face and study it. Like before, I know he's middle-aged and deeply afraid. The lines of his face are smooth, so he's probably someone who spends most of his time indoors. Doing things that are perverse. My stomach rolls in disgust at what those things might be.

Other than my own disgust, I don't see

or feel anything in particular. What is it Silas wants me to see? Frustrated, I turn back to him and shrug. "What am I looking for?"

He *tisks* at me again, but there is a faint hardening in his eyes that worries me. "Emma Rose, if you can't see, then you will not be able to defeat Deleriel, and all will be lost."

Even for Silas, that sounds ominous. I think Deleriel scares the bejesus out of him like Silas does me. Which ratchets up my own terror a notch or three. Anyone who frightens Silas is not someone to mess with. Yet he expects me to "deal" with him. But how? I'm lost, truth be told. I have no idea how to deal with a demon. I deal in ghosts, not demons. That's more along the Malones' line of work.

I let out a frustrated sigh. I don't know what he expects me to do here. It's only a man on a table. Afraid and helpless, but still only a man.

"Death unlocked your reaping abilities, and fear did the same for your demonic side, but I don't think it will work for the other half of your abilities." Silas taps a finger to his chin as he thinks. "She warned me of this, but I had no idea it would be this difficult."

"She?"

"Your mother," he says absently. "How do I wake up the one ability you must be able to utilize in order for any of this to work?"

"Melissa told you…"

"No, not Melissa, your mother." He cuts me off, a frown on his face.

"Melissa, or Georgina, or whoever you want to call her *is* my mother, Silas." What is he going on about now?

"Did I not just tell you there isn't anyone on this plane of existence who could do what Deleriel needed?"

I nod, not understanding what he's trying to say.

"Georgina Dubois was just the body that housed your mother."

What? That makes no sense. "I don't…"

The room is hazy and I blink, trying to focus, but my vision blurs, and before I can say anything else, the world goes dark around me.

Chapter Six

The steady beeping of machines wakes me. I've gotten so used to the sound, I'm not even surprised anymore. The soft light coming from the bathroom sends shards of pain ricocheting through my skull the minute I open my eyes. They seem to be more sensitive to light than the last time I woke up. It takes me a second to remember why I'm here. Seizures. They admitted me because of seizures, and Silas…Silas!

Silas dropped a bomb on me, and then I'd been pulled out of his little retreat. I guess my subconscious started waking up or something. Either way, I am in a world of trouble. Demon, reaper, and something else. Something that's not from this plane of existence. Well, demons and reapers aren't from here, but what else could it possibly be? What type of power is required to bring images to life?

Those questions are swirling around in my head when I hear the creaking of the leather chair that's been pulled up beside my bed. I crack an eyelid and glance sideways. Eli. A little slide further to the right and I see Dan passed out cold in the other chair. He doesn't look well. In fact, he looks about as bad as I feel.

"Hey, sleepyhead."

Eli's voice is quiet, hushed. I'm guessing to keep from waking Dan.

"Hey." My voice sounds like I've been sick for a week and hacked up a lung. "Can you close the bathroom door? The light…"

"Sure, sure, Hilda. Gimme a sec." Footsteps sound across the room and I hear the door shut. This time when I open my eyes, I'm not assaulted by daggers. The room isn't pitch dark. He's left enough light to make out shapes, but I'm grateful for that much. The headache pounding behind my eyes makes me wonder how sick I really am. I've never felt pain like this before.

"Here, take a sip. Not too much, though." Eli holds a bottle to my lips and lets a little bit of water tip into my mouth. The cotton balls coating my tongue are washed away, but leave behind a bitter taste. "You scared us, Mattie."

Ohh, he's using my name. I must have really scared them for him to resort to that.

"Sorry." I blink, letting my eyes adjust to the near total darkness. "How long was I out?"

"Three days."

What? Three days? No way. It felt like I was only with Silas for an hour, at most. I was there for two days with him? Well, maybe not, but he did say he called me there to protect me, so maybe. It's confusing.

"Zeke called in three big hotshot neurosurgeons." Eli sits on the bed, pushing my legs a little to make room. "You had a brain bleed, Mattie. That's serious. It had to be recent because it wasn't on your earlier head CT."

I don't remember hitting my head, but then again, the entire cemetery adventure is a big blank for me. I might have done it there. I'll have to ask Kane the next time he shows up.

"That's what was causing the seizures?"

Eli shifts closer. "No. The doctors are stumped, but Zeke thinks it has something to do with the ghost kids that keep attacking you."

"I…" A coughing fit interrupts me and Eli presses the water back to my lips. I drink greedily, my sore throat grateful for the cool liquid. I turn my head, and pain knifes through it. "Owwwee." I glance to Dan to make sure I didn't wake him, but he's still out. He needs the sleep.

"Don't do that, Hilda." He leans over and helps me sit up a little then adds another pillow behind me. "You just had major brain surgery. It's a miracle you're talking at all."

They had to open my skull? My hand automatically goes up, and sure enough, I can feel bandages around my head. They cut me open? Before I can freak out, Eli grabs my hand and squeezes. "Calm down, Hilda. You and Dan now have matching war wounds."

The panic recedes and leaves only a calm feeling behind. I know as soon as Eli's gone, it'll all rush back. His sense of calm and reassurance lasts only as long as he's with me. Stupid Guardian Angel bond. It should work better than that.

"How did you convince them to let you stay?" Last I knew, Dan would have body checked his brother if he tried to get near me because of the curse. Heather, Eli's mother, is afraid the curse will confuse Eli's Guardian Angel bond as true love and he'll attempt to kill me. I've seen what happens to the women who have loved his ancestors with those beautiful aqua eyes. I lived through their deaths, thanks to my shaman abilities that let me see things.

"I'm your Guardian Angel, Mathilda Louise Hathaway. There isn't a force on this Earth that could have kept me away while you were in danger. Your dad recognized that the minute he saw me. I freaked Ava out, I think. She said I glowed." A chuckle escapes. "Now, that, I would like to do on Halloween. Best costume ever."

"You were glowing? Did anyone see?"

"Only supernaturals can see supernaturals, Hilda. Regular humans...they're blind when it comes to those of us with special abilities."

Well, that makes sense. I'd never met anyone who could see ghosts until Doc introduced me to the Malones in New Orleans. If people saw half of what I did, they'd all be locked away in the nut house on a permanent vacation.

"I'm glad you're here, Eli."

"I'm not going anywhere, Hilda." He leans down and presses a soft kiss to my lips. "You owe me a date, remember?"

This time, there are no butterflies swarming around when he kisses me, only a sense of dread. He doesn't know what I am. Eli despises demons. What's he going to say when I tell him I'm part demon?

"Hey, what's wrong?" he whispers, his voice tickling my ear.

"I have to tell you something, Eli."

Best to get it over with. Besides, Eli knows me. He knows I'm not evil. He's not going to denounce me and try and stab me. I'm Mattie Hathaway. I'm awesome.

"Mattie, you need to rest, honey. You look ready to fall asleep any second." True concern bathes his voice, but I need to tell him. I hate secrets and lies, and keeping this from him, it feels like a secret.

"I'll sleep in a bit. Promise."

"Okay." He sits up and stares at me. Even in the dim light, I can see his eyes. They are bright, intense.

"Couple things I found out about my mother's side of the family, and Zeke's too, I guess."

"They're criminals just like the Cranes?"

Part of me wants to snark at him over that, but I bite it back. My father's family are criminals, but they're *my* family. It is what it is.

"My mother's real name is Georgina Dubois."

"Dubois?" He says the word slowly,

and I know the wheels are turning in his head. "The Louisiana Dubois family?"

"Yes."

"They're pretty scary people, Mattie." A frown worries his lips. "Scarier than even your dad's family. There are rumors…"

"I know." I cut him off. "The rumors are true."

"You can't know that."

"I do." I squeeze his hand. "You remember when you asked me what was wrong with my eyes? When they went black?"

He nods. I can barely make it out, but I push on. "I'm part demon, Eli."

"No, Mattie, you're not." The denial is swift and adamant. "You wouldn't have been able to get past the demon-proofing Caleb did…"

"Did his spell cover humans who have demonic abilities?" His silence is my answer. "That's what I thought."

"Hilda, you're not a demon." He jumps up, his eyes wide. "You're not a filthy demon!"

I wince, but stay quiet. He's not taking

it well at all. "There's more."

"More?" His voice is incredulous. "How can there be more?"

"Silas is my grandfather."

Eli simply falls into the chair next to Dan's and stares at me. I can sympathize. I still feel a mixture of disbelief and horror at the thought.

"Silas has been selectively breeding people on both sides of my family to produce me. He created me to finally deal with Deleriel."

"Do you know how insane that sounds?"

"Yeah, Eli, I do, but it's the truth. I have to figure out how to tap into my abilities so I can defeat a fallen angel or suffer the consequences."

"Consequences?"

"Silas has no qualms about what he'll do to me and the people I love if I don't do exactly what he wants."

"All those times he did stuff for you without asking for anything in return...it was because he was your family?"

I shrug. "I guess. I don't know why he does anything."

"You're a demon."

The empty, hollow sound in his voice scares me. I wish I could see his face better, but the darkness in the room prevents that.

"Zeke thinks I only inherited demonic abilities, that I don't actually have the demon bloodline in me." Though, if I'm being honest with myself, I know that's hogwash. You can't have demonic abilities without having demon blood coursing through you.

"I need to go." He stands and shoves his hands in his pockets. "I need to think…"

"Eli."

He shakes his head at me. "I need to think, Mattie."

Without another word, he turns and walks out the door.

Pain lashes at my heart, the calm and peace giving way to despair. He left. He just left. A tear trickles down my face, and I brush it away angrily. He walked out and left me.

"Shhh, Squirt." Dan's fingers slip through mine. "It'll be okay."

"He left."

Dan stands and pushes me over, climbing into the bed. He pulls me against him. "It's okay, Mattie. Everything will be okay."

"Everybody leaves me, Dan."

"I didn't." He hugs me to his chest. "And I never will."

Chapter Seven

~*Dan*~

I slip out of the bed once she's finally asleep. She'd cried herself out. Eli had better be gone, or he and I are gonna have words. So, she's part demon? Who cares? Anyone who knows Mattie knows she doesn't have an evil bone in her body. She even believes in God and all that. The girl is religious. Prays and trusts that everything happens because of some grand scheme the big guy upstairs has mapped out. Me, I don't know if I buy into that. But it doesn't matter what I believe. It matters what she believes.

I eavesdropped. I admit it, but if I'd known the crap my baby brother was gonna pull, I'd have tossed him out before she had time to open her mouth. Not that I wasn't just as shocked as Eli when she told him Silas was her grandfather. That demon scares me. Terrifies me, really. He's the reason I almost died. And he's her grandfather.

The waiting room is empty save for the Cranes. Eli must have told his family. Disgust and contempt boil in my stomach. I don't care who or what she is. She's just Mattie to me. She's more my family than the Malones will ever be, and if they can't deal with her, demon blood and all, then that's too bad. I'll pick Squirt over any of them.

"How is she?" Zeke looks up from his laptop when he spots me.

"She woke up a while ago."

"Why didn't you come get me?" Zeke closes his laptop, his expression turning irritated.

"I had to calm her down." I put up a hand to stop his questions. "She told Eli about the demon blood in her family, and he didn't take it too well."

"So that's why they all hightailed it out

of here." Josiah Crane, Zeke's father, hands his wife, Lila, a Starbucks coffee cup. "I saw them all piling into a truck when I left to go ferret out some drinks."

"She's sleeping now." I rake a hand through my hair. I really need to get it cut before I see my mom again. She'll nag me about it being too long. "I need to run home, take a shower, and get some clean clothes. Can someone sit with her? I don't want her to wake up alone."

"Of course." Lila stands, her perfectly coifed hair falling down. None of them has left the hospital since Mattie was admitted. "Don't argue with me, Ezekiel. You just said if you didn't get some work done, the whole place was going to collapse around you. If she wakes, I will call you."

"Thank you, Mama." Zeke turns his attention back to me. "Dan, maybe you should get some sleep before you come back. You don't look well."

I shake my head even before he's finished talking. "No. I just need a shower. I'll be back." Before he can argue, I turn around and start walking.

There are a few things I need to do now that I know she's okay. I send my dad a text to come pick me up, and I walk outside to wait. No one will let me drive. I'm perfectly fine. Aside from some severely massive headaches.

The next call I make is to James Malone. Time is running out to find Kayla Rawlins—probably already has run out, truthfully. I need the case files, and hopefully James won't hassle me about it. As freaked as I am about this new ability of mine, Mattie's right about one thing. I'll never forgive myself if I could have helped the girl and didn't.

"Malone."

The voice is brisk, abrupt, and more than a little impatient. He must be having as bad a day as I am.

"Hey, James…it's Dan."

"Dan?" My biological father's voice goes from irritated to a hesitant pleased. "How's Mattie?"

"Eli hasn't told you?"

"Told me what? Is she okay?"

Curious he didn't tell his father his girlfriend is a demon, but then again, they destroy demons, so maybe not telling him was the best idea. "She's fine."

"Ah, good." He pauses and mumbles something to someone else in the room before returning to the conversation. "What can I do for you, Dan?"

"I was hoping you could get me copies of all the case files on the missing kids. Eli said you'd taken over the investigation."

"Are you sure you're up for that, Dan? You're still recovering from your attack and…"

"I need to work, James. With everything going on, I need to work. I know I took a leave of absence from the force, but I can still work on this. These kids are coming to Mattie. Her dad thinks they're overloading her brain and it's what's causing her seizures. If we don't figure this out, it's going to kill her. She can't take much more."

"I didn't know."

"It started the night Meg was shot, and the last attack was at her funeral. This one almost did kill her. I need to do something besides sit and wait for the next ghost to appear that I may or may not be able to see."

"Okay. We can use another set of eyes anyway. Grady says you're good. Very good."

Grady thinks I'm good? I respect him more than any other cop I've met. To know he thinks I'm a good cop means a lot.

"Can you swing by the station? I'll have copies made for you."

"My dad's picking me up so I can go home and take a shower and get some clean clothes, then I'm heading back to the hospital. Could Caleb bring them over to the hospital? I need to talk to him anyway."

I'm hoping he might know a way to help me focus this new ability I have. If I can do that, I stand a good chance of picking up some clues on these missing kids. Right now, when I can get an impression from an object, it's mostly a bunch of jumbled images that make no sense.

"I'm sure that won't be a problem." He pauses again, speaking to someone before coming back. "I wanted to say I was sorry I wasn't at the house when you came over. This case…"

"I know. Time's running out. Truthfully, the kid's probably already dead and they just need to dump the body, but if we can stop this from happening to another kid, we have to try."

"You sound like me." He laughs softly. "Caleb and Eli both hate it when I talk like that. They want to find Kayla alive, but he's had her for almost a week. It is more likely than not she's already dead."

"It would be great to find her alive, but it's not practical at this point. Given what we know about the past victims and our perp's timeline, it doesn't look good for the little girl. I'll admit that, but I guess I still want to hope she's alive as much as the boys do."

"As do we all." James sounds tired when he says that. It can't be easy on him, trying to find a kid who's about the same age as Benny, his youngest son.

A horn blares, and I look up to see my dad waving at me from the driver's side of his car.

"Dad's here, James. I gotta go. Thanks for letting me see the files." I hang up before he can say anything. It's rude, I know, but I don't want Dad knowing I'm talking to him. Even though Dad says it doesn't bother him, I think it does. It's just this look he gets. I can't really describe it, but it hurts me to see it on his face.

"Hey, Dad! Thanks for coming to get me." I get in and buckle my seatbelt.

"How's our girl?" He pulls out into traffic and settles back for the short ride to our neighborhood. "I'm assuming she's awake since you pried yourself away from her bedside?"

"She is. Her grandmother's sitting with her so I could take a much-needed shower and get a bite to eat. I stink, which she pointed out right before she fell asleep."

Dad laughs. Mattie always amuses him. She's like the daughter he never had.

"How is she, really, though?" His laughter dies as he gets serious. "I know I spoke with her father yesterday and they were concerned."

"They still don't know what's causing the seizures. Every time she has one, she gets weaker and weaker. If they can't figure it out soon..." I let my voice trail off. No need to state the obvious.

"After surviving everything she's been through, it wouldn't be right to for her to die like this."

"We're not telling her how bad it really is," I say and turn the heat up. I'm freezing. I can't seem to get warm these days. "If she knew, it would just freak her out more."

"Dan, it's over a hundred outside, and you're turning on the heat?"

I shrug. "I'm cold."

Dad gives me a look, but then launches into a discussion on football. He's already gearing up for his fantasy football team. He and I argued heavily about who should be on our starting lineups. Even my brother, Cam, has gotten into a few heated debates with Dad over his picks. He always seems to pick the craziest team, but manages to win almost every single time. Insanity.

When we arrive at the house, I sit there a minute. I haven't set foot in the house since before Silas almost killed me. It's sobering to think I might never have stepped foot back inside it again, or hugged my mom, or played video games with Cam and my nephew when they come over for Sunday dinners. I almost died. Because of Silas.

Who happens to be Mattie's grandfather.

I wince as a sharp bolt of pain lances the area right behind my eyes. I've been getting a lot of headaches and nosebleeds since the night Meg died. The doctors have run several CTs, but they've all been clear. Even while Mattie was out, I had them run another one, but it came up clean. They keep assuring me it's normal after a brain injury to have headaches, and that nosebleeds are common in anyone who's been on oxygen for prolonged periods of time, but something is wrong. I just don't know what.

"You coming?"

I look up to see Dad standing beside

the passenger door. Gritting my teeth at the pain, I get out and follow him up the porch steps and into the house.

"Earl, is that you?"

My mother, Ann Richards, looks up from the kitchen island where she's sorting through recipes. Her blonde hair is pulled back into a ponytail, and she's got on sweats and one of Dad's old t-shirts. She looks like she's about to tackle her weekly cleaning of the house. It's the only time you'll find her not immaculately dressed. She could even give Lila Crane a run for her money when it comes to best dressed.

Except today. In her cleaning clothes.

"Dan!" She smiles and almost trips over her feet to get to me. I let her hug me for a minute then disentangle her. I'm still trying to come to terms with the fact she murdered my birth mother. Dad hasn't gotten over it yet either. I'm lucky they haven't killed each other since I haven't been home.

"You stink." Her nose wrinkles.

"That's what Mattie said." I shake my head. Leave it to girls to point out the obvious. Dad had refrained from remarking on my apparent odor.

Her expression sours at the mention of Mattie. She hates her, blames Mattie for everything. Only none of it is Mattie's fault. She didn't murder anyone. Ann did all that. Secrets have a way of coming out. What she did would have been discovered eventually, with or without Mattie's interference.

"You good to take me back to the hospital after I grab a shower, Dad?"

"Yeah. Do you think her father will mind me going up and checking in on her?"

"Nah. Zeke's cool."

"Cool?" My mom's expression morphs into something akin to rage. "He's a vicious monster, and you think he's cool? You have no idea what he's done…"

"What I know is that he'd do anything to protect his child. I think you, of all people, would understand that, Mom." I don't give her time to respond, but head upstairs to my room. I'd moved out when I started college, but Mom always kept my room intact in case I needed a place to crash. I grab a pair of clean jeans, a t-shirt, and underwear before ducking into the shower.

Once I'm clean, I go back to my room and collect a couple notepads and some pens, as well as my laptop. I hope Dad won't mind swinging by my apartment so I can grab a couple of my dry erase boards to set up in Mattie's room. If she can't leave the hospital, I'll bring the investigation to her. Sometimes she sees things I don't, and I hope it'll take her mind off everything.

I feel so bad for her. Finding out she's part demon and that Silas is her grandfather on the heels of surviving an obsessive psychopath? She's had a bad break the last few weeks.

Helping me with the investigation is just the thing she needs.

Downstairs, I find my mom buried in the fridge and a sandwich waiting on the island.

"Mom, is that for me?"

She jumps a little at the sound of my voice. "Who else would it be for?" When she straightens and closes the door, she turns with a bottle of cold water in hand. "Here. You'll need this."

"Thanks." I sit and dig in. My stomach rumbles appreciatively. It's been a while since I've eaten. I think Zeke made me eat something yesterday, but I honestly can't remember.

"Dan, I'm worried about you. You don't look well."

I know that, but not a lot I can do about it.

"I'm fine, Mom."

"No, you're not fine, Daniel Aaron Richards."

I wince at the use of my full name and her mom voice. Never bodes well.

"You suffered a major brain injury then checked yourself out of the hospital. There is no way you're fine. Your father tells me you're having headaches and nosebleeds on top of that."

"I had a head CT. It was clear. Really, Mom, I'm all good. Don't worry so much."

A heavy sigh leaves her. "I'm your mother, Dan. It's my job to worry about you. Which is why I'm concerned that you're spending so much time with Ezekiel Crane."

"Mom, I'm not getting into this with you." I put the sandwich down, appetite gone. "Mattie is a part of my life, and since he's her father, he's part of my life too. I know he's a bad guy, I do. I'm a police officer. I researched him. He's still her dad, though, and he loves her."

"There are things the internet won't tell you, Daniel. Things that would cause you to run screaming…"

"Things like kidnapping a pregnant woman, holding her hostage until she gives birth, and then savagely murdering her?"

I regret the words the second they leave my lips. Her face goes white and she clutches her throat with one hand. I know how badly I've hurt her, but she needs to understand that as bad as Zeke is, she's done some pretty awful things too.

"Dan, what I did, I did to save you. Those people, they are evil."

"Why are they evil, Mom? They don't seem evil to me."

"That's because you don't understand who they are, what they can do…"

"I know who they are, what they can do," I interrupt her. "I know it because I can do the same things they can. Does that make me evil too?"

Her white face turns ashen. "I thought if I took you, raised you away from all that, it would be different, you'd be safe."

"Enough!"

We both flinch at the roar of Dad's voice. He stalks over to us, wagging his finger. "I am sick and tired of hearing about how evil the Malones are, Ann. I've met them all. They are not evil. They are nice people who are dealing with this situation with grace and understanding. Dan is not evil because he's James Malone's son. I don't know and I don't care what imagined evil you think they are guilty of, enough is enough. I will not have my son think he's some kind of leper because of your insanity."

"I'm not insane."

"Then you explain to me what caused you to murder an innocent woman." The pain in his voice is enough to make me ache for him. He loves my mom so much, but he's having a hard time accepting and forgiving what she did. I didn't realize how hard until just now.

And no matter what she says, he'll think she's insane. I know she's not, at least when it comes to the world of the supernatural. Dad has no idea. He's still living in the fairytale world of the normal humans who think ghosts are just scary stories you tell kids around a campfire.

"Dad, she's not crazy."

"Dan, I know you want to protect your mother, but enough is enough."

"No, Dad, she's not insane. Ask around about the unit James Malone works for. Then ask yourself how insane she is."

He frowns, clearly wanting to argue the point, but I simply don't have the energy for a fight. I don't want him accusing Mom of being insane either. At least if he starts poking around asking about the spook squad of the FBI, he might start to understand all is not as it seems.

"I need to get back, Dad. Are you

ready?"

He nods, and I don't give him time to change his mind. I stand up and go hug my mom. "I'm sorry," I whisper. "I love you, Mom."

"I love you too." The gratitude in her eyes makes my guilt all the worse. I shouldn't have brought up what she did to make her shut up about Zeke. Warranted or not, it had hurt her, and I won't do it again.

Once we're in the car, I lean back, exhausted. Who knew coming home for a quick shower would turn into an emotional ordeal? I should have guessed it, though, given Mom's feelings on the Cranes.

Instead of focusing on that, I pull out my phone and start going over the notes I'd jotted down about the missing kids. One list includes abduction and dump sites. The third child had been found in the park two blocks down. The forensic tech Mattie and I talked to said they hadn't looked for the black goo that smelled like sulphur and had been found on Kayla's bear at any of the other sites.

No one knew to look for it until that point.

An idea forms and I look over to my dad.

"Hey, Dad, you up for a side trip?"

Chapter Eight

Freedom Park has always been one of my favorite places. Even after I got too old to play, I still went there just to think. It was only two blocks from my house, and I frequently used the batting cages to work out frustration. As we pulled in, I did notice there weren't that many cars here. Nothing like finding the body of a child to deter parents and teens alike. This wasn't New York City. We weren't used to dead bodies turning up in our parks.

"What are we looking for, son?"

I glance over to my dad. His eyes are scanning the park, alert, but curious with just a hint of excitement. Earl Richards is a detective at heart, whether he'll admit it or not. My brother, Cameron, became an attorney just like my dad and my grandfather, but I went to the police academy. Mom flipped out, saying it was too dangerous, but Dad? He had the biggest grin on his face. I think I fulfilled a secret fantasy of his. He's a closet cop.

"We found a black substance on Kayla's bear. When I asked forensics about it, they didn't know what it was and admitted they hadn't looked for the black goo at the other sites. I just want to check to see if it's here."

"Black goo?"

"Best description I have, Dad. It smells like sulphur." I get out of the car and start walking. They'd found the body of Carl Dowling about fifty feet from the third baseball field.

"Do they have any leads on who's taking these kids?" Dad hurries to keep up with me, and I slow down, remembering he's not as young as he used to be. Sure, he's only fifty-two, but he does have high blood pressure, and Mom's always nagging him to slow down.

It's not long before we come upon the area that's still roped off with police tape. James Malone had requested it remain sealed until his own team could comb through it. I know for a fact that request upset quite a few at CMPD, including the forensics team. It rubbed them the wrong way when the FBI came barreling in and insinuated the cops didn't know what they were doing by going over all their work.

"Are we allowed in there, Dan?" Dad gestures to the area. "It's still taped off."

"I'm a CMPD officer, Dad. I'm allowed." I duck under the tape and stand there, taking a moment to study the area. The ground is littered with footsteps. There always seems to be more people at a crime scene than necessary. It can screw up evidence. We all know it, and yet it still happens. There are very few who will order unnecessary uniforms behind the line. Had Sergeant Carver, head of our forensics department, been here, he'd have ordered them out. He'd been at the abduction site of the next victim while his guys handled the dump site of the last victim.

I haven't seen the crime scene photos, so I'm not exactly sure where the actual body was, so I start walking slowly, scanning everything. Broken leaves and twigs have blown over the area. We'd gotten a big wind storm recently. No rain, just wind. The weather guy called it weird. Best he could do. Granted, a massive windstorm in the middle of one hundred degree heat with no rain *is* weird. I wonder if it has anything to do with a soul-sucking demon.

At the very edge of the perimeter, closer to the woods lining the field, I see it. Black droplets on the ground. If I hadn't been looking for it, I would have missed it. They're tiny, like ink stains. I squat to get a better look. Touching before forensics has a chance to collect the evidence is a no-no. I won't tamper with evidence. I lean down and take a big whiff, and the smell of rotten eggs assaults my nose. Sulphur.

"Did you find something?" Dad calls from where he's practically falling over the tape. I shake my head and suppress a laugh. He looks like some crazed fan at a concert trying to get the musicians' attention by leaning so far over the line, they'll fall at any second.

"Yup, I did." I send James a text, as well as Detective Grady, who's in charge of the case at CMPD. Then I snap a picture of the droplets with my phone. That done, I stand and scan the area again, but there's nothing left to find.

My phone rings, startling me. James Malone's name flashes at me, and I answer it, shooting a glance at my dad. "Hello?"

"Dan. We found Kayla."

"Where?"

"At her school. One of the other kids found her sitting on the swing."

"Sitting? Is she..."

"No," James cuts me off. "She was posed. Sorry, I should have phrased it better. She's a mess. Worst one yet. The medical examiner is here along with CMPD forensics, and my team collecting evidence. I thought you might like to come over and see the crime scene for yourself while it's fresh."

My gut twists. This is going to hit Mattie hard. She liked that little girl. A lot. And for Mattie, that's saying something. She doesn't like most people.

"Yeah, sure, I know where it is. Dad's with me, though. Is that okay?"

"It's fine as long as he stays out of the way. See you when you get here."

The call is disconnected, and I shove the phone in my pocket. The man never says goodbye. It's different. My parents always say goodbye to me before they hang up. Granted, I had hung up on him earlier, but hanging up on people seems normal for James.

"Dad, you up for one more side trip?"

"What's wrong?"

"They found the little girl who was taken from Mattie's neighborhood."

Dad turns grim. He's a parent. I'm thinking every parent in the Charlotte-Mecklenburg area tonight is going to be paranoid and paralyzed with fear. The body's been found, which means the next victim will go missing within twenty-four hours if they haven't already been taken.

***

Kayla's school is swarming with black and whites when we get there. I have to flash my badge to get through. Dad's eyes are everywhere, drinking it all in. He's never seen this side before. Sure, he's seen crime scene photos. He's a defense attorney, after all, but to see it up close and personal while it's happening? He's like a kid in a candy store.

"Just stay close, Dad." When we park and get out, I wind my way through the crowd that's swarming the police tape. Officer Chris Jenkins is standing guard at the entrance. I know him from the Academy. He was also at Kayla's the day she was abducted.

"Dan." Chris nods to me when I finally reach him. "You see the press? Vultures."

I glance over at the area where all the news vans are parked. Reporters and cameramen are prepping to go live. This is not something Mrs. Rawlins needs to see on the evening news. Chris got it right when he called them vultures. Picking away at the dead, digging at people's hurt.

"Agent Malone asked me to come look at the body." When Chris's eyes flicker to Dad, I introduce him. "This is my dad, Counselor Earl Richards. He's with me today."

"I don't know." Chris hesitates. "We're not supposed to let anyone but the police behind this line."

"I'm still having some head trouble man. I'm not supposed to go anywhere alone. Dad's here in case I pass out or something. He won't get in the way and he won't touch anything. You have my word."

His face scrunches up in indecision.

"If there's any heat, I'll take it."

After a long moment, he nods and steps aside. For a minute there, I thought I might to have to call James to get us in. Well, Dad, anyway. "Thanks, man."

"Dan." Chris's tone stops me more than anything, and when I turn around, his face is grave. "It's bad. Worst one yet. I hope you haven't eaten."

Now I regret the sandwich I ate. I give him a nod of thanks, and together, Dad and I navigate through the sea of people. The crime scene itself is relatively clear of people, but then I see Sergeant Carver bent over something next to one of the swing sets. He's put the extra uniforms to good use too. There is a wall of blue around the crime scene. Even if the reporters wanted to get a shot of the body, they couldn't. The men lined up surrounding the area prevents it.

I spot Caleb and head in his direction, careful to keep my eyes averted from the swing sets. I'll look at the body, but for now, I want to get as much information as I can before I do.

"Caleb."

My brother looks up at the sound of my voice and waves. His eyes flicker to Dad, but he doesn't make any comment. Caleb is a carbon copy of his father, and in turn, me. There is no denying we're brothers. We look too much alike. Mattie told me he reminded her of me before she knew we were brothers.

"Hey, Dan." His deep voice is quiet, the somberness of it relaying how bad the situation is. "Dad said you were coming.

You're sure you're up to this?"

"I'm fine. CT scans are clear."

"I know. I was there when the doctor told you. That's not what I meant. You and Eli haven't gotten much rest in a couple days. How's Mattie, by the way?"

Huh. So Eli hadn't told Caleb or James about her heritage? In a way, that's a good thing. We need her help to solve this, and I don't want anyone second guessing her because of something she has no control over.

"She's awake, but that's about all that's changed. She had another seizure last night."

"After everything that kid's been through, she doesn't deserve this." Caleb lets out a heavy sigh. "Now this? She knew the little girl, didn't she?"

"Yeah. Her next door neighbor's granddaughter. So, what do we know?"

Caleb glances towards the swings then quickly looks away. "Not much. CSU is processing the scene right now. Once they're done, we can get in for a better look."

"James said the body was posed?"

Caleb's face darkens. "She was tied to the swing so she wouldn't fall off. She looks like she's sitting there, ready to push off. Her lips are gone, so they drew a huge smile on her cheeks with a red marker. Rigor has come and gone, so she's been dead for at least a day. We'll know more once they get her back to the morgue."

"How long ago did they find her?"

"About two, two and half hours." Caleb checks his watch. "The school said she wasn't there any earlier. They've had several classes out here all morning, and it was the last class of the day who found her."

"Witnesses?"

He shakes his head. "No. We've got people canvasing the area, but it seems he just magically appeared, had enough time to pose *and* tie her up, then magically disappeared."

"How long between classes coming out for recess?" Dad asks, tilting his head.

"Thirty minutes or so, why?"

"That's plenty of time to do it."

When he looks doubtful, Dad laughs.

"I'm a defense attorney, Caleb. It's my job to figure out what's possible, and then debunk it. Trust me when I say thirty minutes is more than enough time to do this and slink away."

"Earl's right." We all jump at the sound of James Malone's voice. He's standing not more than a few feet behind us. How he'd snuck up on all three of us, I don't know. He's as stealthy as Mom's cat. I hate that animal. She loves to startle me then stare me down.

"Carver's wrapping up now. He says we can go in any time. It's gruesome." He looks at Dad when he says this. "You might want to stay here."

Dad hesitates. I know he's torn between wanting to see a real live crime scene and thinking about the nightmares it'll give him. Some things you just can't unsee.

"You should probably stay put, Dad. We don't want a defense attorney having any ammunition to get evidence thrown out on a technicality, and a civilian on scene could do it."

"You're right, of course. We don't

want this monster getting off because the defense might claim I touched something or tainted evidence."

None of us remark on the evident relief in his voice. Instead, we go over to where Carver is talking to one of his techs. I'm taking forensic science classes at North Carolina University. Carver is the reason I decided to go that route. I don't know a better cop, even if he only looks at the physical evidence. Nothing gets past him. He has an eye for detail, much like Mattie does.

"Agent Malone." Carver nods toward us as he closes his notebook. "The scene is all yours."

"Did you find any of the black substance I asked about?" James takes out his own notebook, ready to make notes. Caleb and I both pull out our phones. I'm assuming he's going to record the conversation as well as take notes. It's what I'm doing.

"Yes, we did. Over by the east gate that backs up to the neighborhood. Just a few drops, though. Strangest thing I've ever seen. Smells like sulphur. Not a common substance, especially in this area. We've run a few tests on the original sample from the girl's bear, but so far, we're getting inconsistent results."

I'm not surprised. It's from a demon. I doubt there's a substance like it on this plane.

"Preliminary?" James turns his head, looking directly at Kayla perched on the swing. He's no longer talking to Carver. He's speaking to the medical examiner for the county.

Angela Moore is in her late thirties, pretty with dark blonde hair and green eyes. She's all business, though. Hard to talk to and always direct and to the point.

"At this point, I can't directly point to a cause of death. She has so many wounds, and any one of them could have been the fatal one. I'll know more once I get her on the table. I'd like to get her off the swing and in transit as soon as possible."

"We'll be quick."

When James moves, I get my first real look at Kayla Rawlins. She's seven, blonde hair, and big, beautiful blue eyes.

That's what she looked like the day she was taken. This little girl barely resembles her. Her face is broken, bloody, and bruised. One of her eyes has been gouged out, the other staring blankly at us. There are deep gashes along her arms and legs, like someone raked a knife up and down them in a precise pattern. Heavy bruises dominate her skin. One hand is missing, the other has missing fingers. Her feet...I look away for a moment. Her feet are barely attached to her legs, only a thin strand of ligament holding each in place. Her white skirt is more of a reddish brown color, blood stains covering it. Her princess t-shirt is pristine against all the other marks on her body. It's clean, freshly laundered, I think.

James squats down and uses his pencil to lift the shirt, and we all hear his gasp. Her stomach is a torn, bloody mess. Parts of her organs are sticking out through several wounds.

How is the shirt so clean? My mind focuses on that instead of the gory mess in front of me. She hasn't been dead that long. There should still be some fluids present.

"CSU needs to run an analysis on her shirt. Someone took the time to wash it." I squat next to James, forcing myself to look at the maze of wounds on her chest and abdomen.

"Policy is to bag each item separately then hand them over to the senior forensics investigator on the case." Dr. Moore's brisk voice interrupts me. "Procedure will be followed."

"Yes, Dr. Moore, procedure will be followed," Sergeant Carver assures her. "I think Officer Richards was more or less making a note of it."

She nods then bounces up off the ground. "Please be efficient, Agent Malone. I need to get started on the autopsy with all due haste." And with that, she picks up her bag and walks away.

James scowls at her retreating back. Our medical examiner takes some getting used to, but she's wicked smart. I wouldn't want to be on her bad side.

"Carver, send everything over to the

FBI lab once you've processed it." James turns his attention back to the body, dismissing the sergeant. Carver frowns, but otherwise says nothing. Not a lot you can say when the FBI hijacks your case and the captain orders you to defer to them. He packs up his things then goes over to where his crew is processing the east gate, leaving us alone.

"It's odd that a demon would take the time to wash her shirt." Caleb keeps his distance. He's not police or FBI. He just graduated college and James wants him to join the Bureau, but I don't think that's what Caleb wants to do. He would have joined the first class after graduation, but he hasn't. There have been two since May. I know. I checked, thinking about it myself. Before I knew about James Malone and his affinity with the Bureau.

"That's because a demon didn't do it." I use my penlight to pull her shirt down around her neckline. There are a few more droplets of the black goo there. The small spot on her otherwise pristine shirt had caught my eye. "He's using a human to torture the souls to the point he can feed."

"How could you possibly know that?" James leans closer, inspecting the drops I'd just uncovered.

"I saw it." I explain to James about my new ability and how I'd used it to touch Kayla's bear and "see" what had happened to her in those last minutes before she was taken. "I'm hoping Caleb may be able to come up with a tattoo or something to help me focus it and make sure I don't see random stuff every single time I touch someone or something."

"I'll research it," he promises then brings the conversation back around to Deleriel. "Demons have been known to use host bodies while on this plane, but usually because they don't have the juice to hold a corporeal version of themselves. I would think Deleriel has enough power to be himself. I've seen him."

"Yeah, but you're not thinking about all the little demons he's created. They need to feed too. He's not just taking kids here in Charlotte. I guarantee if we do a nationwide search, you'll find the rate of missing kids has spiked over the last two months. He's corralling his children food, while he's using someone here to collect *his* food." It's a theory, but one I've thought a lot about and am almost one hundred percent sure I'm right.

"That does make sense." James nods slowly. "He could go find his own monsters food, and when this soul is ready, he could siphon some of his energy back into the host and feed if he were busy elsewhere. It's the only way he could be in two places at once. And it does make sense. Locklier!"

A young woman, maybe twenty, twenty-five rushes over to us. Her dark red hair is restricted in a severe bun, and her brown eyes are sharp, bright with eagerness. A new recruit, maybe? She seems overeager.

"Sir?"

"Locklier, this is Officer Daniel Richards. He's just given us a clue we didn't know we had. Deleriel is using a human to do his work here in Charlotte while he's out rounding up food for his army of child monsters. Do a nationwide search, concentrating on the states closest to us, for a spike in missing children. Within the hour, Locklier."

"Yes, sir." She nods then rushes off in much same fashion as she arrived.

"She new?"

James laughs. "You would think so, but no. She just has a lot of pent-up energy and is always rushing around like a whirlwind. Dan, do you think you could give us a description of the man Deleriel is using?"

"I only saw him for a minute, and he was blurred with Deleriel's image, but I can try. I do need to get back to the hospital, and if Mattie isn't up for doing the drawing, I'll call CMPD's sketch artist."

"No, don't do that. It'll bring up too many questions about how you got your information. I'll have our resident artists come to the hospital and do the sketch. It's best to keep all this to ourselves. The less CMPD knows, the better."

I hadn't thought about that. I don't want anyone I work with knowing what I can do, especially since I'm having a hard enough time accepting it myself.

"Dan, if you were to touch the body now, do you think you'd get anything?"

James's question snaps my head back around to stare at him. "What?"

"Dad, there's all kinds of people here. Trust me, it's not something normal people will understand." Caleb says exactly what I wanted to, but was too shocked to utter. James wants me to touch a dead body? Doesn't he realize what I could see? The torture...no. Some things even I won't do.

"No, James, I won't do that for the same reason I told my dad to stay back. Some things you can't unsee."

"Even if it means helping us to capture the person who did this?"

"Dad, don't. He's not ready for any of this. He wasn't raised like we were."

James purses his lips, his eyes narrowed. "Think about it, Dan. I can get you access to the body when you're ready."

I stand up and back away. "I really need to get going. If you can have copies of everything brought to Mattie's room, I'd appreciate it. Talk to you then,

Caleb."

Without another word, I walk as fast as I can away from James Malone and his request. I'm not ready for any of this, and I won't be pushed into it.

I'm a cop, yes, but I also have a sense of self-preservation, and seeing what was done to Kayla would haunt me to my dying day. I won't do that to myself.

I'll focus on what I do best, and that's at looking at the evidence, putting the clues together, then tracking down the bad guys based on good old-fashioned police work.

It's what I do.

Chapter Nine

~*Mattie*~

I feigned sleep to get everyone out of the room. I'd woken up to my grandmother instead of Dan. Not that I'm not glad she was there; I just missed Dan. I'm used to him being around when I wake up, but I did tell him to go home and get some new clothes. He stank in a bad, bad way.

I heard Josiah say they were dragging Zeke home to change, and then they were all going to get dinner before coming back. Which means I have at least a couple hours of peace and quiet. I know Zeke's concerned about ghosts since he can't very well salt doors and windows in a hospital. Not a lot you can do, though, unless you want the staff to think you're certifiable.

My headache is gone, at least. I think that has more to do with the drugs they gave me than my getting better. They've already dragged me down for no fewer than three CTs over the last few hours. I'm not sure what they think is going to change in a few hours, but I guess it makes them feel better to be doing something useful.

I'm not concerned about dying. Silas said he wouldn't let me die, and I trust him. He has plans for me, and dying isn't a part of them.

I let out a hollow laugh. A demon has plans for me. Never in my wildest dreams could I conjure up this scenario. Sure, I see dead people, but demons? Throw in angels and Lord knows what other kind of supernatural beasties out there, and it's *Supernatural* hyped up on super mega steroids.

All I ever wanted was to have a family and be a normal person.

Well, I have the family, but I have

accepted I'll never be normal. If I can just survive, I'll count it as a win.

"Finally, you're awake!"

I look up to see my foster sister, Mary Cross, breeze into the room, her long honey blonde hair pulled up in a loose ponytail. Her tone might be light and airy, but the worry in her blue eyes belies her easy attitude. Her mom must have warned her about my condition. It's not an easy thing knowing the next seizure could kill you. I still haven't let myself dwell on it.

"For the minute." I yawn. Sleep seems to be pulling at me when I'm awake. The body's way of trying to heal itself. "You and me, we're gonna have words."

She frowns and plops down in the chair next to the bed. "What did I do?"

"Let's see, how about failing to mention you had a run-in with Deleriel, and now he seems to want to take you back down under with him?"

Her eyes go wide. "What? He said no such thing. Who told you that?"

"Silas told me. He may be a lot of things, Mary, but he's not a liar. Deleriel intends to have you. What did you do to get the attention of a fallen angel?"

"Nothing!" Her eyes squint as she thinks. "I was just protecting Noah."

"How did you protect him?" Mary might be able to hear ghosts, but she's in no way supernatural. She's very much a human. It never made sense to me how she stopped him, but we'd not gotten the chance to talk about it either, circumstances being what they were.

"I stood up to Deleriel and told him he couldn't have the baby. I wouldn't let him."

"You stood up to a fallen angel?" My sister is a hundred times braver than I am, but that is probably what caught the demon's attention. I shake my head. She did the right thing, but it probably sealed her fate.

"What?"

"Mary, no one stands up to him, not even Silas. Until you."

"You think if I'd let him eat the baby, that would have been better?" The outraged fury on her face makes me almost feel sorry for Deleriel. When

Mary gets pissed, people flee in front of her.

"No, I don't think you should have let him eat the baby." I can't help the sarcasm. When I get scared, I get snarky. It's a defense mechanism.

"Then what else was I supposed to do?" she asks angrily.

The pain starts right behind my left eye. Stress headache. "There's not a lot you could have done, Mary. I know that. I just wished you would have told me about it sooner."

"Mattie, you were at your dad's getting ready for the party. I was going to tell you when I saw you there. Then you and Meg went missing and..." She lets her voice trail off. Then Meg died. She doesn't have to say it. I went home with Zeke, and when I got back to her house, she didn't have time either, what with Kayla going missing and all.

I rub my eye trying to ease some of the stabbing pain. "I know, Mary. I'm sorry, it's just I'm worried. Deleriel...I don't know how I'm supposed to defeat him, and thinking he might escape with you?

It just adds an extra layer of fear to all this."

"Why does it have to be you, Mattie?" She leans forward, propping her arms on the mattress. "Let the Malones deal with it. It's what they do. You just concentrate on getting better."

"I wish I could." I give her a rundown of everything Silas had told me, including the part about him being my grandfather and Eli's reaction to it.

"Well, that's going to make for some fun Christmas dinners."

"You don't care I'm part demon?" I glance at her face out of the corner of my eye. She doesn't look disgusted or horrified. In fact, she's smiling.

"You're my sister, Mattie. You could be the devil's child himself and I wouldn't care. You saved my life. Not just down in that basement either. You helped me through the months after we escaped. You understood and never let me sink so far into depression, I didn't come back from it. That was all you. You're the best person I know, and if Eli can't see past his own racism, then that's all on him. He doesn't deserve you."

"Racism?"

"Sure. He's racist against demons and anyone with demon blood. His problem, not yours."

"But demons are evil, Mary…"

"You stop right there!" She wags her finger at me. "You are no more evil than I am. You are the opposite of evil. You're good and kind, and you love bigger and harder than anyone I know. Don't you dare call yourself evil."

"I love you, Mary Cross."

"I love you too, sister mine. Now, no more talk about Eli and his racist beliefs. Tell me something good."

"I met my grandparents."

"I know, so did I. They seem pretty awesome. Although, your grandmother looks a little scary."

"They kind of are awesome. Lila can be scary too. She tried that with me and got nowhere."

Mary laughs. "I bet."

"Zeke wants me to go to New Orleans with him."

"What?" She sits up and eyeballs me.

"New Orleans?"

"I've been thinking about it."

"Why?" She sounds more curious than angry. Dan had all but blown up on me.

"No one knows me there. No rap sheet to worry about. No one staring at me with pity because of everything that's happened to me. No reminders of Mrs. Olson and that basement. It could be an honest to goodness chance to start over with a clean slate, Mary."

"Then you should do it."

I glance up, startled at the conviction in her voice. She's staring at me, but she's not. It's more like she's staring through me. "If you have the chance to try to put that basement behind you, then you should. I hear you at night, crying in your sleep, begging her to stop. If you can escape the nightmares, then you should."

We'll never be able to escape the nightmares. All the therapy in the world isn't going to erase what happened to either of us down there, trapped with a madwoman bent on torturing us. Mary isn't the only one who hears things. I hear her screaming at night, crying out. I don't know if anyone can ever truly get past something like what happened to us. It scarred our souls.

"Why don't you come with me?" The look of longing in her eyes prompts me to pose the same question to her that I did Dan, but for an entirely different reason. "We could both start over in a place where we're not reminded every day about that basement."

And we are. Every time Mary goes for a walk, she sees that night in the rain when Mrs. Olson hit her with her car and took her. Every time I think about foster care, I'm reminded of Mrs. Olson. Not all of my foster care memories are bad ones, but here in North Carolina? All I think about is Mrs. Olson. I obsess about it. I always try to figure out why I didn't see the signs, why I didn't know something was off with her. I should have known and been better able to protect myself.

"To New Orleans?" Mary looks stunned.

"No, to N'awlins." I draw the words out exactly like Lila. "Don't let my grandmother hear you say it any other way. She gets pissy about it."

"I don't know, Mattie. My mom's here, everyone I know is here. It would be harder for me to just up and move away like that."

"I know, but think about it. It could be good for you, to get away from here, from the memories." The door swishes open and we both turn to see Mary's mom come in, chart in hand.

"Mary, honey! I didn't know you were here." She starts writing numbers down. "I thought you said you had a date later tonight."

"Date?" I give her a sly look. "A date with Caleb, perhaps?"

"Yes, a date with Caleb." A blush steals across her cheeks, and her mom chuckles. "He texted earlier, though. Said he might have to cancel. His dad has him doing something."

"Then you can come keep me company tonight." I yawn. "Protect me from the grandparents coddling."

"Let them coddle you." Mrs. Cross ruffles my hair, much the same way Caleb does. "It makes them feel better."

"I know, I just need to get used it, I guess."

"Mom, how would you feel if I went away to school?"

Mrs. Cross pauses, her hand frozen on top of my head. "Go away?"

Mary bites her lip. "Yeah, I know I took some time off, but I've been thinking about college a lot lately."

"You were all set to go to NCU before...before the incident."

"That's just it. Mattie and I were talking about everything that happened to us. It's hard to be here, Mom. Every day it's hard to get up and not think about what happened. I think maybe going away for a while might help me."

Mrs. Cross sits on my bed. "Mattie, do you feel the same way? Is it hard for you too?"

I nod. Leave it to Mary to tackle this headfirst. She's blunt. More so than even me. "Therapy can only do so much, Mrs. Cross. For me, North Carolina is one big horror story. Just being here brings up memories of all the bad things that happened to me."

"Girls, I don't want either of you to suffer. If being here is causing you pain, then you should go."

"But what about you, Mom?" Mary tilts her head. "What would you do if we left?"

"Same thing I do now." Mrs. Cross smiles. "Get up, go to work, fend off the crotchety old men who come in from the old folks' homes. Maybe try Match dot com?"

"Online dating?" Mary scrunches up her nose. "I don't know about that now."

That prompts a laugh out of her mother. "Where are you girls thinking of going?"

"My dad wants me to go to New Orleans with him. I'm sure he can get Mary into Tulane or LSU."

"This close to the semester starting?" Mrs. Cross looks skeptical.

"Mom, her dad has money, and he's from New Orleans. I'm sure all he'd have to do is make a phone call."

I nod, ignoring the pain it causes. "That's true."

Mrs. Cross is quiet for a long time, just

sitting there thinking. It freaks us both out a little. Mary worries her bottom lip with her teeth while I drum my fingertips against the mattress. When she speaks, it startles us both. "I love you girls, and I'll miss you, but your wellbeing is more important to me than anything. If going away will help you deal with the nightmares, with the memories, then I am all for it."

"Really?" Mary leans back, not expecting that.

"Girls, I can't say I won't miss you, but you're both growing up. You need to start learning to be adults, and that means I need to learn to let you make decisions. Part of being a parent is knowing when to let go, and if this helps you deal with the incident, then you should do it. Now, I have to go down the hall and check on Mr. Muncy."

"Isn't he the one who always tries to pinch the nurses on the behind?" I remember her complaining about him.

"That he is." She laughs and gets to her feet. "Neither of you worry about me. You worry about yourselves. I'm happy as long as you're happy."

Once she leaves, I turn to face my sister. "Are you sure about this? It means leaving everything behind, including Caleb."

She frowns, but shrugs. "Caleb is complicated. His dad is pressuring him to join the FBI, but he doesn't want to. He wants to go to medical school. I think he should stand up for what he wants, but he seems to think he should put his dad's wishes before his own. Family business and all that."

"You two seem to really like each other, though."

"I do like Caleb a lot, but I don't want someone who lets others make decisions for him, decisions that'll make him bitter later. Caleb needs to do what he wants, or he'll regret it for the rest of his life."

"Well, maybe on your hot date tonight you can broach the subject with him. Tell him you've decided to go to college in New Orleans and maybe suggest he apply for medical school down there or something. It's not like we can go until I deal with Deleriel, anyway. He's here, not in Louisiana. Silas will never let me leave until I do what he wants."

"That's not at all fair."

"Nope, but what choice do I have?" I shrug, dismissing the subject. "You best get home and get cleaned up for your hot date. And I want details."

Another blush covers her cheeks in a blanket of cherries. "You get some sleep, Mattie."

There's a gentle knock on my door, and I look over to see Mrs. Owens, Jake's mother, rolling Jake into my room. He looks better, even if he's still in a wheelchair.

It's not Jake, though. It'll never *be* Jake. I dumped Eric, AKA Mirror Boy, into the shell that used to hold the soul of Jake Owens, my ex-boyfriend. He'd also saved me the night his psycho brother Paul tried to kill me. He'd been shot in the process, and his soul passed on, leaving his body alive for any willing soul to enter.

"Hi, Mattie. We heard you were here, and Jake wanted to come see you. Are you up for some company?"

She's beaming. In the span of five minutes she'd gone from deciding to take Jake off life-support to having him wake up. She and her husband know something's not right, but they don't care. They have their child, and that's all that matters to them.

Jake's now blue eyes regard me curiously. Eric had the bluest eyes I'd ever seen, and Jake's were brown. When Eric's soul entered Jake's body, his eyes took on the color of Eric's. Why, I don't know. Another question to ask either Zeke or Doc. I'm just glad to have my Mirror Boy back.

Eric was the first ghost I met who could hurt me. He'd been trying to protect me and didn't know he could cause me physical harm. We'd become friends during my time as Mrs. Olson's torture victim, and he'd stayed with me, refusing to let me die alone. He'd left only once to try to show Dan where I was. Thankfully, he'd succeeded, and Dan found me before I died, but Eric had stuck around, saying I needed someone to keep me out of trouble. He'd later sacrificed himself to save me from a very nasty ghost, and I'd reaped him, which allowed me to transfer his soul into Jake's empty body.

He gives me a hesitant smile. "Hi."

The first real smile I've had all week crosses my lips. Eric always makes me smile, and even if he never remembers who he is, that simple fact will never change. "Hi."

"Is it okay that I came? They said you were really sick, so if you're tired or something, we can come back…"

"No, it's fine." I sit up and adjust the bed. "I could use some company that's not my grandparents and Mary was just leaving anyway."

"They're just worried." Mrs. Owens wheels Jake/Eric over to my bed as soon as Mary gives me a quick hug and heads out.

"I know. I'm just not used to so many people fussing over me, I guess."

"I am going to go down to the cafeteria and grab some dinner. I should be back in forty-five minutes or an hour. Is that good?"

"That's fine, Mrs. Owens."

As soon as she's out of the room and the door closes, Eric gives me the biggest grin. "I didn't think she'd ever leave."

I frown. He sounds like the old Eric, but last I checked, he had no memory of being Eric.

"Eric?"

"Who's Eric?" He tilts his head questioningly.

"An old friend of mine. I miss him."

"Why did you call me by his name?"

"Sorry, I was just talking out loud. Your mom being a little too clingy?"

"God, yes. I just wish they'd all leave me alone." He runs a hand through his hair and grimaces. Jake's hair is very short. Eric had longer hair. I think, deep down, he knows it's supposed to be long, even if he doesn't know why. "I feel bad when she's here because I don't know her and she's trying so hard. Showing me pictures, telling me stories. I don't remember anything about being Jake."

"I'm sorry. I know it has to suck not having any memories."

"But that's just it. I do have memories.

Of you. They're blurry, but they're there. You're the only thing or person I can remember. And that name you just called me...Eric...that feels like *my* name, even though they said I'm Jake."

"What kind of memories?" Hope springs to life inside of me. Maybe he will remember who he is if the name Eric is familiar to him.

"You sitting on this tweed sofa flipping through a magazine. Then another time, you making dinner for some little kids. Then you falling to your knees, your hands over your ears, in a lot of pain."

He's remembering me at my old foster mother's, Mrs. Olson's. Eric had been her first victim, and hence he was tied to her. Falling to my knees in a lot pain? First time I realized a ghost could hurt me. Mirror Boy had nearly killed me with his psychic attack.

"Then it kind of blurs and doesn't make a lot of sense. I've seen flashes of you with your hands broken, of you running from someone, and of you surrounded and bathed in this white light. Crazy, I know, but like I said, they're weird memories, like from a dream or something."

"Why don't I tell you about my friend Eric? He saved my life, you know. Twice."

"He sounds like a real stand-up guy."

"He is."

And so I tell him the story of Mattie and her Mirror Boy. I leave out the ghost part, but I tell him everything else. I tell him how he stayed by my side through the worst moments of my life, how he came to my rescue in New Orleans. I give him the rundown on everything, hoping to spark his memories.

"Wow. He sounds like Superman or something."

"Or something." I grin down at him, remembering the time I'm pretty sure he spied on me in the shower, but couldn't prove it because he'd been a ghost at the time.

"Mom says you and I dated?"

I laugh. "Yeah, we did for a couple months."

"I had to be an idiot to let you go."

"I'll agree with that."

"I'm sure you would, Hathaway." He gives me that cute grin that is all Jake Owens, dimples and everything. It makes me catch my breath, a wave of grief taking me by surprise. Jake and I were friends, and he's gone now. Sitting here, chatting with Eric, makes me realize how much I will miss Jake.

"Hey, what's wrong?" He reaches out and takes my hand, and then the strangest thing happens.

His eyes roll back in his head, and I open my mouth to scream for help, but this soft white light surrounds him. From head to toe. I'm so shocked, I forget to call for help. He does a full body shiver then his eyes snap open, the blue stark against the white he's bathed in. Only there's no hint of confusion in them this time.

"Jake?" I whisper, hope refusing to be squashed.

"Mattie? Where...where are we, and why are you calling me Jake?"

Oh my God, oh my God, oh my God. "Eric?"

"Yeah?"

I lunge toward his head. It's all I can really hug since he's sitting in a wheelchair. "Thank you, thank you, thank you." I chant the prayer of gratitude over and over. It's Eric. It's really him.

"Hey, now, Mattie. What's going on? What's wrong, and why are we in the hospital, and why can you hug me?"

I pull back and look at him, really look at him. It's Eric. He's right there. The eyes really are the windows to the soul. I can see his soul reflected in them. "You're alive, Eric."

"What are you talking about? Did you hit your head again or something?"

"No, I…well, yes, I did hit my head again, but that's not the point. Do you remember Jake Owens? My ex?"

"Surfer dude?"

"What? No, he was not a surfer dude."

"Could've fooled me with that perfectly combed hair of his. Always styled just so." Eric flips his hand back toward his hair and smacks his head. His expression freezes. "I felt that. I shouldn't be able to feel that. I'm a ghost,

Mattie. Ghosts can't smack themselves."

"That's because you're not a ghost anymore. It's what I'm trying to tell you."

Eric sits back and really looks at himself for the first time. He's sitting in a wheelchair, wearing a pair of pajama pants I'm assuming Jakes's mom brought from home and a white t-shirt. He holds his hands out in front of him and tentatively touches his fingertips together. He has an IV needle taped on his right arm, ready to be used should he need more fluids at any time.

"What's going on, Mattie?" He runs his hands over his arms then touches his face. "I don't understand."

"Do you remember New Orleans?"

"Jonas…he was trying to siphon your ghost energy?"

"Yeah, and you made me reap you so I would have enough energy to fight. I've had your soul bound up inside me since then." I touch my hand to my chest. "You've been right here with me ever since."

"But…"

"Let me explain, okay? Do you remember Mason?"

"The guy I body jumped so I could kiss you on your birthday?" He grins, his unease forgotten for a moment with the memory.

"Yes, that Mason. He wasn't a very nice guy. He had a problem. Bit obsessed, really. So was Jake's brother, Paul, only his obsession was Meg. The two of them kidnapped us. Jake showed up, wrong time, wrong place, but it saved our lives. Paul shot his brother, and we were able to run in the aftermath."

"Dang, girl, you been busy."

That's an understatement. "Anyway, an angel showed up and he wouldn't let me bring Jake or Meg back. I'd already saved Dan and upset the balance of life and death as it was. Little bugger threatened us all if we tried to save them."

"Angels?" He gives me a skeptical look.

"What? No worse than the demon who seems to think I'm his new toy."

"Seriously, Mattie? Angels and

demons?"

"Ghosts are real. Reapers are real. You're looking at one. Wraiths are real. Why shouldn't angels and demons be real?"

"Next you're going to tell me there are vampires and werewolves roaming around."

"There might be. I don't know about that. Eli says there's a lot more to the supernatural world than we know, so…"

"Wait, who's Eli?"

"My kinda-sorta-maybe boyfriend."

"Kinda-sorta-maybe? He's either your boyfriend or he's not. Do I know him?"

"No, you don't. I met him in New Orleans at the house. He sees ghosts too, only he can see vengeful ghosts, the ones who go bad."

"Are you talking about Blondie?"

"Blondie?"

"Blond hair, sea green eyes Blondie?"

"Yeah."

"Thumbs up, then. He's hot." His face flames up and his eyes go wide. "Why did I just say that? I don't think guys are hot."

"Maybe Jake did, though?" Which would explain a lot. He was just too perfect of a boyfriend. Never argued, never yelled, always had a great sense of fashion. Never pressured me to have sex with him. Oh my god. That really would explain so much.

"Well, I'm not Jake."

"Pfft, there's nothing wrong with liking guys if you want to."

"I didn't say there was anything wrong with it. It's cool. People should be happy with who makes 'em happy. I just like girls, that's all."

"Okay, then. I'm good with you either way." The disgruntled look on his face tells me he's going to have to do some adjusting. Jake's residual memories and tendencies are there, and Eric will have to deal with them one way or another. I know for a fact Eric is straight, but if Jake wasn't, then it could cause some problems for Eric in the future, or it might lead to possibilities he never would have looked at before. Then again, he can be straight, gay, or bisexual, for all I care. I'm just glad he's here. Alive and well.

"Let's get back to Blondie. How can he be a kinda-sorta-maybe boyfriend?"

"Well, we haven't even been on a real date yet."

"Girl, don't tell me your game disappeared."

"No, it didn't. There's just been a lot going on." I give him the rundown on the Malones being Dan's family, how my mom is mixed up in it, the ghost girls who tried to kill me, and I give him a more in-depth explanation of the night Jake died. "So as you can see, I haven't had time to go on any dates."

"Just listening to all that makes me tired." He shifts and winces. His hand automatically goes to his abdomen where he feels bandages. "Forgot for a second, he got shot. This hurts. A lot."

"Well, deal with it. You're alive, and that's all that counts. Plus, the Owens' didn't lose both their sons. All is well with the world."

"They don't know I'm not Jake, do they?"

"No, they know something isn't right. I mean, Jake's eyes were brown and now they're blue. That's not something science can explain, but they don't care. All that matters to them is you're alive and well."

"But I'm not Jake, Mattie. I'll never be Jake. I don't know who he is or who he was. I don't know his family, his friends. How can you expect me to pretend I'm him when I'm not?"

"Eric, you and me, we didn't have family growing up. We were just numbers in a system, checks to be collected by our foster parents for the most part. Every foster kid dreams of a forever home, of people who will take them in and love them the way they deserve to be loved."

"Yeah, but…"

"Shush. No buts. Jake's parents don't care if you have no memories of them, and they don't care that you're different from the old Jake. All they care about is that you're their son. They *love* you. It's what every foster kid dreams of. You get that now. You get parents who will unconditionally love you. All you have to do is give them a chance. Let them love you, and you might get the greatest gift in return. A family. A family you'll love as much as they love you."

"She's right."

We both jump at the sound of Mrs. Owens's voice. She's standing by the bathroom door. How had I not heard the door open or seen her sneak in? I really am off my game today.

She comes closer and kneels in front of Eric. "I don't care who you were or who you are now. I don't care if you never remember us or your old life. You're my son, my *flesh and blood*. We'll get to know each other again, learn to love each other. I'm willing to try if you are."

"But what if I'm never like the old Jake again? What if I'm too different?"

"Then I'll love the new Jake." She smiles, and it's written right there on her face. She loves him. It's hard to walk away from that kind of unconditional love. It's something Eric has never known.

"Hey, look at me. I have a dad and grandparents and everything. I don't know them from beans, but they love me, and that's the most amazing feeling in the world. Something I thought I'd never have, and now that I do, I would fight tooth and nail to keep it. It's precious...Jake." Dang it, I almost said Eric. "Your mom's right. All you have to do is try."

He bites his lip, his dimples deepening as he thinks. "I guess I can try. I just don't want you to be disappointed or to feel like you're being cheated or lied to..."

"No, Jake. I will never feel like that. I know my son died. The version of him I knew died that night. We'll never get him back. I understand and accept it, but the person sitting here right now? I have a feeling we'll love this person just as much as we did him. That we'll make new memories and learn each other's quirks as we get to know one another. It'll be an adventure."

"You're pretty awesome." His voice holds more than a hint of awe. Everything he's ever wanted is being offered to him on a silver platter. All he has to do is reach out and take it.

"I'm a mom, nothing more, nothing less."

"Okay, then. We'll try."

She smiles and leans into him, hugging him tight. Her eyes meet mine, and I know she knows the truth. She heard every word. It's stamped all over her face, and she doesn't care. Not one little bit. She'll love Eric as much as she loved Jake.

Thank you, she mouths at me.

Thank you, I mouth in return and mean it. She overheard our conversation. She could have reacted so many different ways. Instead, she chose compassion and love, and because of it, Eric has a family who will love him like he deserves to be loved. He'll get his forever home.

"What say we get you back to your room before that nurse hunts us down?" Mrs. Owens stands, brushing tears from her eyes. "Mattie probably needs to rest too."

"I am a little tired." And I am. I'm worn out, truthfully. Whatever I did to bring Eric's memories back sapped my energy. I know I did something, I'm just not sure what. That white light is the same thing Dan described to me when I put Eric's soul in Jake's body. This whole reaping business is tiring.

"All right...Mom, let's let her rest." He points at me right before she turns him around. "But me and you, Hathaway, we got to talk more about this whole kinda-sorta-maybe thing and your lack of game."

"You don't even know the half of it." I shake my head as they leave the room, feeling at peace for the first time since Eric died. All is right with the world.

"Such a beautiful moment, my darling girl."

My head snaps up at the sound of that voice.

Silas.

Chapter Ten

Silas walks over to the bed, and it's all I can do not to cringe. He looks like he's in a bad mood. No, scratch that, he looks pissed. But is he pissed with me? That's the real question.

"Silas." I do my best to keep my voice steady and calm.

"You ran away before we were finished, Emma Rose." His black eyes center on me, and I know then he's pissed with me. Not good, not good, not good.

"Not my fault, Silas. I can't control when I wake up out of an unconscious state."

"I suppose I have to accept that." He comes closer and examines the machines

I'm hooked up to. "These seizures are going to kill you, Mathilda Louise Hathaway. Sooner rather than later."

He's using my full name, the name I grew up with. Why? It instantly sets off my flight or fight instincts, and right now, flight is screaming the loudest. Wait. Did he say kill me? Does he know something the doctors don't? Or is everyone keeping the truth from me? Silas is a psychotic, self-serving demon, but he's not a liar.

"I could prevent that." His voice turns cunning, like a weasel about to enter a henhouse. "With a simple touch, I could fix you."

Now what's he going on about? He told me he wouldn't let me die because he needed me to complete his end game, and he wants something in return for keeping me alive? Demons. Always trying to get a better deal.

"And what would your price be, Silas?"

"Oh, I don't know. You'd owe me a favor, much like the one you called in when young Officer Richards needed saving."

"Why would I agree to such a deal, Silas? I already know you won't let me die. You said as much. So what's really going on?"

"Keeping you alive is not the same thing as making you better, my darling girl. I can keep you in a state of flux for as long as is necessary. I can even train you in my studio while you lie here unconscious." He tilts his head, his eyes brightening. "Why, yes, that is an ideal solution. I know your body will be safe, and your soul will reside with me until you are ready to confront our mutual enemy."

And he could do it too. I can't be alone with him for God knows how long he deems it necessary. I won't.

"Over my dead body."

Eli.

Only a version of Eli I've never seen before.

He storms into the room, his eyes blazing with the fires of Heaven. His body is lit up, pulsing with a white light that blazes around him, its heat all-consuming. Power rolls off his skin, crackling with vengeance. I can feel it. The kind of power you sometimes feel in a church when you are alone, sitting there quietly praying, only magnified a thousand times.

I never really understood what it meant to have angel blood in your veins until this moment.

Even Silas takes a step backward.

"Get thee gone, thou vile beast." His voice has changed, deepening and resounding through the room. Heat lances us, and I shield my eyes from the glow he's bathed in.

"Emma Rose, meet your Guardian Angel." The smile on Silas's face sets my teeth to aching. Did he do all that just to get this reaction out of Eli? Why?

My gaze flicks to where Eli is standing. He's shining so brightly it hurts my eyes to look at him, and I turn away. He's lit up like a Christmas tree, oozing holy fire.

"Even if he doesn't want to be your Guardian Angel anymore."

Eli flinches at Silas's words. Is Silas

right? Do I disgust Eli so much now that he doesn't want to be my Guardian Angel? Hurt flashes through me, settling in my heart.

"I will always be her Guardian Angel." Eli moves, inching closer to Silas. "She is my charge, and I will protect her with everything that I am. Come near her again, and you'll see exactly how far that protection goes."

Silas laughs. Outright laughs. Eli has amused him. "That little display of power is like a tickle. You need to sit before you harm yourself, boy."

Eli might be shining like the holy warrior he is, but Silas is right. He's just a boy, and Silas has centuries on him. "Eli, calm down. Please."

"Yes, watchdog. Sit." There is a definite bite to Silas's voice this time, and a command as well. Eli refuses to back down. He sidesteps the foot of the bed and gets closer to Silas.

"Eli, please don't."

His head whips around to face me. "Protecting your family?"

A stab of pain ricochets inside my head

like a ping pong ball on steroids. "No, I'm protecting you, you idiot. He could swat you like a fly. Now, *please* calm down. Silas isn't going to hurt me. He did that to get you riled up. Why, I don't know." I turn my attention to the resident demon. "What gives, Silas?"

Usually I wouldn't dare upset him, but I need to know why he got Eli hopped up on Guardian Angel juice. He's up to something.

He shows me an expression so innocent even a child would have a hard time coming up with it. "Whatever do you mean, my darling girl?"

"You made him go all warrior crazy with your threats. Why?"

"What will you give me for the answer?"

"Nothing."

"Then you'll get no answer."

We stare each other down, neither blinking. The heat level in the room is receding, so I know Eli is finally calming down.

"How did you know Eli would be here?"

"He can't stay away. As long as you are in danger, he has to be close."

I look to Eli and he nods, the glow around him dimming to a point I can actually look at him. "Ever since the day at the cemetery, I haven't been able to go more than a few miles from the hospital for very long."

And he resents it. He doesn't need to say it. The flinch I'd seen earlier when Silas made that remark...that said it all.

And just like that, it clicks into place for me. Silas tested him. He knew Eli left earlier, walked out when I told him I had demon blood in my genealogy. Silas needed to make sure he'd still protect me.

"You do please me, Emma Rose. So very much."

The glare I shoot him is hot enough to scorch the flames licking the inside of his eyes. "That was unnecessary. I can take care of myself. Always have, always will. Mattie Hathaway needs no one to protect her. Got it?"

He slinks to the head of my bed and pats me on the head like a small child who's throwing a tantrum and he's indulging me. "Yes, my darling girl, I know you can take care of yourself against most things, but Deleriel is not most things."

"Deleriel?" Eli's voice has gone back to its normal tones, and when I glance his way, he's no longer glowing, but his eyes are still bright, intense.

"Yes, Deleriel." Silas strokes my hair as he speaks, and I find it oddly comforting. My mom used to do it when I was scared, and it would always make me feel better. No one's done that since I was five. "He'll be coming for her soon. I may be one of the most powerful demons among the Nine Circles of Hell, but even I am not a fallen archangel. My protection spell won't last much longer."

"Deleriel feeds off children. Why would he want Mattie?"

"He grows tired of his prison, and she is the key to his freedom."

"I don't understand." Eli crosses his arms, watching Silas like a hawk, like he expects him to do something to hurt me at any second.

"Because she possesses the one gift he

covets, the one gift that will allow him to breach the veils between the planes of existence and stay here on Earth. He will be able to come and go as he pleases, no laws or restrictions to hinder him."

"Her reaping ability?" Eli asks, clearly confused. "If that was the case, couldn't he go out and find any reaper?"

"No, young hunter, it is not her reaping abilities he is after, it is something else entirely."

"Then, what?" Eli growls. "I can't keep her safe if I don't know what I'm dealing with."

Silas warned me to tell no one about my gift. And I followed that advice. Dan doesn't even know. Eli already sees me as an abomination. Telling him this could put the nail in my coffin with him.

"He's right, child. He needs to know. Now that I know he will protect you, it's safe to tell him."

Silas actually reminds me of Zeke right now. He's being very family-oriented, soothing my nerves by stroking my hair, acting all concerned about my welfare. If I didn't know him any better, I'd think he cared.

But I do know him.

"My blood can breathe life into images." I sneak a peek at him, and he only looks more confused than before.

"I don't understand, Hilda. What does that mean, exactly?"

"Silas, will you please hand me my sketchbook?" I point to it sitting on the little tray they put your dinner on. Josiah had brought it to me, thinking I'd like to have something to do while I was here. I'd spent the last several hours sketching the man I'd seen lying on Silas's table.

When he hands it to me, I flip it open to that particular image. It's a perfect replica of him. It shows his pain, his fear, all that emotion is etched into the lines of the drawing.

"Your talent is remarkable." Silas leans closer, examining it. "Once you figure out how to see past the outward mask to what resides below the surface, you'll be ready."

"I still have no idea how to do that."

"But you will, my darling girl, you will."

I ignore his cryptic promises and look around for something to draw blood. Realizing what I need, Silas takes my hand in his and uses one of his claw-like fingernails to puncture my index finger. I almost tell him thank you, but why would I thank him for drawing blood? Instead, I pick up my charcoal pencil and dip it in the drop of blood that has welled up.

With the image of the man firmly in my mind, I add a little more detail to his eyes, and when I'm done, I lean back and look down. The picture has done exactly what I expected it to do. It starts to move, to come alive. The eyes so expressive I can feel the pain radiating out of them. The image is alive, his essence trapped there for an eternity.

Eli sucks in a breath when he sees the lines of the drawing move and bend, the emotions forever trapped on the surface of the paper. His eyes devour the image, and he sticks out one finger, about to touch it, when Silas slaps his hand.

"Don't touch." Before either of us can say anything, he snatches the sheet right out of the pad and folds it before tucking it into the pocket of his suit coat.

"How does this help him to stay here, though?" Eli sits at the foot of my bed, clearly disturbed by the drawing, but willing to push it down until he gets answers. "Not to say that it isn't amazing, but it's still just a drawing."

Silas shakes his head, irritated, but Dan answers for him. "It's not the drawing, but the intent behind the drawing. If he can draw a doorway with the intent to leave it open, and bind it with his blood, then he can do as he pleases."

Silas beams at him. "Clearly, young Officer Dan inherited the brains in the family."

Dan moves into the room, and I see a subtle change in him. His aura is different. Brighter, more intense. Just as intense as Eli's was a moment ago, but more controlled, more contained. Dan's is actually scarier than Eli's little display of power, because of how subtle it is. I look closer, and much to my surprise, I see the outline of a sword strapped to his back. The Sword of Truth? I know he gave it to Mr. Malone to keep it safe, but

I can clearly see it. Does he even know it's there?

Silas does, though. He retreats to the window.

"You okay, Squirt?"

"Why wouldn't I be? I mean, I have my Guardian Angel on one shoulder and the devil on the other. Every girl's dream."

"Don't be snarky." Dan leans down and ruffles my hair. "You okay?"

"I'm fine, really."

"What are you doing here, Silas?" He leans against the railing of my bed, arms crossed, much like Eli had earlier. Only when Dan does it, it's much more intimidating. Maybe it's because he's older than Eli, but I don't think so. I think it's more to do with Dan's new status of Warrior of God, holder of the Sword of Truth.

"Coming to make sure our girl doesn't die, of course. These pesky seizures are going to be the death of her."

Dan's eyes narrow. "You can heal her?"

"Yes, but only for a price."

"We're not making any deals with you, demon." Eli snarls.

Dan stare at Silas, his expression measuring. "You *can* heal her, though?"

"I'm not making a deal with him, Dan, and neither are you." I will not let him make a deal with a demon. I don't care if it could save my life. He's not selling his soul. "If you do, I swear to God, I will never speak to you again. Promise me, Dan. Promise me right now you will never make a deal with Silas."

He purses his lips. "But if he can help you…"

"I mean it, Daniel Aaron Richards. Promise me."

"Fine, I promise." He doesn't sound at all happy about it, but I sit back, satisfied. Dan won't go back on his word. It's not in his nature.

"He forgot to mention he already told me he's not going to let me die. He needs me."

"For what?" This piques his curiosity.

"To stop Deleriel for him."

Dan's face falls, and I know something's wrong. "What happened?"

"We found Kayla Rawlins."

"No." All the breath whooshes out of me. That little girl is a kid I know, someone I took time out to play with. She was such a sweet kid. Her grandfather and her mom must be devastated.

"We have less than twenty-four hours to find the human he's using before they take their next victim."

"If they haven't already," Eli mutters. "Hold on. Did you say the human he's using?"

"We are off topic, children." Silas claps his hands to regain our attention. "We must focus on stopping Deleriel before he finds Mattie. She needs to learn to use her gift, to unlock the last door in her mind that will allow her to truly see."

"The last door?" Dan pulls up a chair and sits. He's wearing that patented bored look of a police officer, but I know better. He's taking in every detail.

"Emma Rose is the perfect trifecta of power. I made sure of it. She's unlocked her reaping abilities, thanks to Amanda, and she opened herself up to her demonic side, thanks to you, Daniel. The very real idea of losing you ripped that door off its hinges and it gave her the power she needed to fight off a full-fledged reaper. There is only one other door, and I'm having problems unlocking it."

Our conversation from the dream comes back. "Earlier, you said Melissa was just a vessel for my mother. What did you mean?"

"Georgina Dubois, for all physical intents and purposes, is your mother. You are made of her flesh and blood, but that is where it ends. You remember I told you Georgina came to me seeking help to deliver what Deleriel needed? I told her the same thing I told you. What she wanted could not be born of any creature on this plane of existence."

"But what does that mean?"

"That, I cannot tell you, Emma Rose. It is something you must discover for yourself."

I swear I want to throw something at him. He can't just toss out little cryptic pieces of information and expect me to accept it.

"Is she like us?" Eli asks. "Part angel?"

Silas barks out a laugh. "Gods, no. What Emma Rose truly is, is more powerful than anything that's walked this Earth in millions of years."

"Why won't you just tell me?" It would be so much easier.

"Because I can't. I would if I could. I made promises, Emma Rose, and as I've told you before, a demon's word is his bond."

"Okay, so is there anything you can tell us?"

Silas nods. "I approached the being and explained to her what I needed. She owed me a favor and had not been on this Earth for a very long time, and so agreed."

"Did she know what Georgina wanted with a child?"

"No." Silas looks horrified at the thought. "She still doesn't know her child was meant to be a sacrifice."

"And if she did know?" Dan asks.

"You don't want to know. There isn't a rock Georgina could hide under."

"Could she stop Deleriel?" If she can, why hasn't Silas approached her?

"I honestly don't know." He shakes his head. "I have tried many times over the last few years to contact her, but she's gone into hibernation. It is what they do when they suffer a wound so deep, it devastates them. Meeting Ezekiel, giving birth to you, staying with you for the first year of your life, then to have to leave? It was more than she could bear, I think. She loved you, but she had to give you up. That was the deal. And deals cannot be broken."

My mind whirls with questions. Zeke said he had no doubt Melissa loved me. He told me she would sit and watch me sleep for hours as a baby. Then she slowly changed, and he began to fear for my life. She changed because she was no longer the same woman. She wasn't Melissa anymore. She became Georgina Dubois. The woman who was going to sacrifice me to save herself. It all makes sense now.

"So it's the gift she inherited from her...*mother* that will defeat Deleriel?" Eli shifts on the bed, turning so he can face Silas. I know he doesn't like having

Silas in a positon where he can't see everything he's doing. Simply being in the same room with him and not trying to kill him is a task for him. His family hunts down ghosts and demons and God knows what else. He's behaving…at least for the minute.

"No." Silas rubs his fingers together in irritation, the sound screeching through my already pounding head. It reminds me of the sound Eric used to make when he tried to scare me, like nails being ground up and crying out in protest. "Did I not just say she is the perfect trifecta? She must be able to use all three of her gifts to defeat Deleriel."

"And you can't tell her what the third gift is?" Eli grouches. "Don't you think it would be so much easier if you told her?"

Again, he's repeating what I thought, what would make me happy. This bond has my feelings for him all confused. If it was just the bond, though, why do I feel like someone's crushed my heart into a thousand tiny pieces and then fed it through a wood chipper? There have to be real feelings there.

In a flash, Silas is right beside Eli. He's moved so quickly none of us saw it. He has Eli by the throat and lifts him up off the bed. "My patience is wearing thin with you, young hunter. If you keep making me repeat myself, I will punish you."

"Put him down." Dan leaps from his chair and has his sword in his hand. I don't even think he's aware of it, but Silas is. He drops Eli like a hot potato and backs away.

"Easy now, young knight."

Dan advances on him, the single intent to harm written in every bunched muscle of his body. It's scary as heck. Silas throws up a hand palm outward, and I feel energy flow out of him and into us. It's enough to slam every door in the room. Eli goes flying backward, but Dan keeps advancing.

"If you kill me, the protection spell on Mattie goes away, and Deleriel will be in this room within seconds."

That makes Dan pause. He glances my way, and it's all the hesitation Silas needs. He poofs. As is his habit. He just poofs away. Leaving a very angry Knight of the Sword in his wake.

Eli approaches him slowly. "Dan?"

Dan whirls, his sword held out in front of him.

"He's gone, Dan. You can put the sword down now."

"I'm not going to hurt you, little brother. I might want to, but I won't."

"Then put the sword down." Eli's voice is soothing, but he's alert. He can't believe Dan would hurt him?

"Sword?" Dan looks down and realizes he's holding the sword the angel gave him the night Meg died. Confusion swamps his expression, and he lets it clatter to the floor. "Where did that come from? I left it with your father."

"It kinda just appeared in your hands," I tell him. "Wicked cool, by the way."

Eli relaxes as soon as Dan drops the sword. "Dad says it will always be there when you need it. All you have to do is reach for it."

"I..." Dan shakes his head, shocked. "It felt weird. *I* felt weird."

"It's the sword," Eli explains. "Dad

says it causes its wielder to crave righteous vengeance. That's why I was a little worried there for a minute. You're mad at me for a lot of reasons, Dan. You have every right to be, but I don't want to end up as shish kabob because of it."

"Eli, no matter how weird that sword makes me feel, I wouldn't have hurt you. For a second there, I wanted to, but I know you're my brother, and there's not a force on this Earth that can make me hurt you. You're family."

Eli nods solemnly. He's right. Dan has every reason in the world to hurt him. Eli was the one who called the cops on his mother. Not that Dan wouldn't have done the same thing, but it was the way Eli did it. I know he wants to make it right with Dan, but I think in this case, it's going to take time. Dan already forgave him; he just needs time to get past it.

"Uh, guys, not to interrupt your Hallmark moment, but what are we gonna do with the sword? Nurses will be in shortly to take vitals, and the Cranes won't be gone much longer."

"Maybe pick it up and see if you can

will it away?" Eli suggests.

Dan gives him a dubious frown, but picks up the sword. The moment his hand touches the hilt, I see the change in him. So does Eli. It's like an entirely new person emerged from beneath his skin. The sword gives him strength, confidence. I feel the power oozing from him. The sword is a part of him now. It's like an extension of him, settling into him like a cat curling up on her master's lap. Dan is the sword as much as the sword now is Dan. He looks downright scary, to be honest.

He straightens and tests its weight, turning it in several different directions. He even tries several jabs with it, and I know I'm right. That sword belongs in his hand. They've melded together, I think.

He looks at the sword, concentrating. "I don't think that's going to work," he says after several long minutes.

"Maybe try to put it back where it came from?" When he looks at me questioningly, I explain. "You pulled it from a sheath on your back, so maybe try putting it back there?"

"I do *not* have a sword sheath on my back." The ire in his tone is unmistakable.

"Yeah, you do, trust me. I saw it when you came in. Just try it. If it doesn't work, it doesn't work."

He's doubtful, but he dutifully tries and almost stabs himself in the head in the process, which produces a giggle from me. Eli barely suppresses his own laughter. Again, it doesn't work.

"See? There's nothing there," he grumbles.

"I think it's more or less you have to learn how to use the sword." Eli pushes off from against the wall he's leaning on. "Just stick it in the closet for now, and then I'll call Dad and see if he can bring over something to come get it in."

Dan nods and puts the sword in the small closet provided in each hospital room. "Caleb is bringing the case files over for me and Mattie to go over. Your dad also wants me to work with a sketch artist."

"Sketch artist?" Eli takes a seat in the

chair Dan vacated earlier. "Why does he want you to see a sketch artist?"

"Because I saw the guy working with Deleriel. When I touched Kayla's bear, I saw him take her." He hesitates for a second, looking directly at me. "I told him I wanted to see if Mattie could do it first, and if not, I'd call his sketch artist."

"I've never actually done that before, Dan. I usually just draw whatever pops into my head. Following directions from someone else is not my strong suit. You know this."

"Yeah, but I had an idea about that." He sounds nervous, never a good thing. "I don't know if it's even possible or if you're up to it, but it was a thought."

"Well, spit it out."

"Whenever I touch you during a ghost attack, I can see the ghost. So I'm wondering if you touch me while I'm thinking about what I saw, you could see it too?"

"I don't know, Dan." I frown, thinking. "A ghost is different from a vision. It's real, tangible. A vision is just a thought or sensory memory."

"Like I said, I don't know if it's possible, but I thought it might be worth a try. You're really good at what you do, Mattie, and I'd trust your vision of the perp better than anything I could describe to someone else."

He had to throw in a compliment, didn't he? My ego preens herself, knowing Dan loves our work, even if it's dark and twisty.

"Dan, I don't know if her brain can handle that kind of mental assault right now. She just had a major seizure. It's a miracle she's awake and talking right now."

"Not such a miracle. I have demon blood in me, remember? I'm betting I'm a little harder to kill because of it. My body can take a hit and keep on ticking."

Eli's face pales, but he nods.

"Do you want to try?" Dan asks, coming to sit beside me on the bed. "It might be risky. Eli's right. Your brain might not be able to handle the sensory overload this could cause."

"Just what are you asking my daughter to do?" Zeke's very angry voice makes us all jump.

We turn our heads to see him standing in the doorway, his face swarming with storm clouds.

"Dan wants her to test their connection." Eli leans back in his chair. "He's hoping she can see what he sees, the way he can when he touches her."

"That amounts to a nuclear assault on her mind." Zeke slams the door shut and stalks into the room. "It might cause another seizure, and we can't risk that. And why does it smell like sulphur in here?"

"Silas was here."

"What?" Zeke turns his attention to me. "Did he hurt you?"

"No." I shake my head. "He wanted to make a deal to heal me."

Zeke's face morphs into rage. "The demon can heal you? He told me last night he couldn't."

"Did you offer him something he wanted, or were you calling in marks he owed you?" Eli yawns, blinking his eyes. I wonder how much sleep he's actually had. Probably about as much as Dan.

"I called in favors." Zeke lets out a sigh.

"Nobody is making a deal with Silas." I'm adamant about this. "No deals. Silas wants something from me. I highly doubt he's going to let me die before he gets it."

"What does he want?" Zeke all but growls the question at me, anger blazing in his eyes.

"Not a clue." The lie rolls easily off my tongue. "He always alludes to it, but never comes right out and says it. He's healed me before, so I'm betting he will again, if necessary. I'm not worried, and neither should any of you."

"And you, Daniel, do you know what the demon wants from my daughter?"

"No, sir. Whatever it is, I think she's right. He's not going to let her die before she does it."

Zeke has this particular ability. When he asks you a direct question, you can't lie to him. It's impossible. Silas, being Silas, forced a spell on me that gave me the ability to lie to my father. He used Dan as a guinea pig to see if he survived it. He almost didn't. That is the spell that put him in the hospital with a massive brain injury. Although it wasn't the spell that put him at death's door. It was the hard hit he took to the head when he struggled against Silas.

The only good thing that came out of it was we can both lie to Zeke without blinking an eye. Dan's gotten much better at lying since he met me. Before, he'd have been nervous, twitchy, and uncomfortable. Now, he's looking Zeke directly in the eye without so much as a blink.

Not sure that's a good thing. I like Dan honest.

Before he can ask Eli, who doesn't have the same protection we do, I blurt out the first thing that comes to mind. "They found my neighbor's little girl."

"*Ma petite*, I am so sorry, *cherie*. I know you were fond of the child."

"That's why Dan was asking me to make a drawing of the guy who took her. We want to stop him before he takes his next victim."

Zeke's lips thin. He's not having it. "I understand, *ma petite*, but it is too dangerous right now. Perhaps I can help in some other way? I have several psychics on my staff who may be able to do what you wanted Mattie to do."

"But can they draw like she does?"

"I do not know, but I can find out."

"Dan, I'm starving. Like, seriously starving. Will you go down to the cafeteria and grab me something? Take Zeke with you and get him up to speed on the disappearances." I want him away from Eli before he asks anything Eli won't be able to lie about. Out of sight, out of mind.

Dan frowns, but he knows exactly why I'm asking him to get Zeke out of the room. As much as he doesn't want Eli near me right now, he can't argue. Eli won't be able to keep the truth of what Silas said quiet.

"I think I should stay, given you've just had a visit from the demon…"

"Eli's with her, Mr. Crane. She'll be fine. I'm hoping your psychics may be able to help us. The sooner we go, the sooner we can get back. If her stomach rumbles much louder, I think she's going to wake every patient on this floor."

"Hey!" Well, it is complaining about my lack of food, but still.

Zeke laughs at my disgruntled face but allows Dan to lead him out of the room.

Leaving me all alone with Eli.

Chapter Eleven

Eli is quiet for a few minutes, watching me. It makes me uneasy. I don't know what he's thinking. It could be anything from I'm demon spawn who should be put out of her misery to I'm the best thing next to chocolate cake. Either way, I hate not knowing. It's unnerving, honestly.

"So, you want to talk?" I can't stand his silence any longer and break it.

"There's a lot to talk about, Hilda. I just don't know where to start."

"Let's start with me having demon blood. That upset you. A lot."

He nods. "Yeah, it did."

"You left, Eli."

"I needed time to think, to process it. I've spent my entire life hunting demons down and killing them, Mattie. Learning the girl you are entrusted to protect, as well as a potential girlfriend, is part demon? That's a lot to swallow."

"But I'm still me, still the same girl you met in New Orleans."

"I know." His voice is low, somber. "It just hit me like a ton of bricks, and I couldn't breathe, Hilda. I had to get out, I had to think."

"Dan didn't leave. No matter what brand of crazy or weird I throw at him, he never leaves me, Eli. *You* left." I can't hide the small hitch in my voice. What he did hurt more than I want to admit.

"Dan didn't grow up like my family did, knowing who and what demons really are. They're manipulative, dangerous, and can make you do things you never thought possible. He doesn't understand demons like we do."

"So since he doesn't understand I'm evil, that's why he didn't leave? Is that what you're saying?"

"No, I'm not saying you're evil, Hilda." He runs a hand through his dirty blond hair. It looks bedraggled.

"Then what are you saying?"

"I don't know." He sighs heavily. "It's complicated."

"No, Eli, it's *not* complicated. Was Silas right? Do you not want to be my Guardian Angel anymore?"

His aqua eyes pierce mine. They are full of so many emotions. "I'm your Guardian Angel, and that will never change."

"But do you want to be?" I press, needing him to answer.

"Yeah, Hilda, I want to be your Guardian Angel. I can't reconcile what I know about demons with what I know about you. You're not evil, Mattie. You're the farthest thing from evil I've ever seen. Demon blood or not, you're not a demon."

Relief snakes through me. He doesn't think I'm evil. That's something, at least.

"And I didn't *leave* you. I just needed time to think. You dropped a live bomb in my lap. Ava and I went to the deli across from the hospital."

"You told her?" I so do not want this to become common knowledge.

"Yeah. She's my best friend as well as my sister, Mattie. Of course I told her. She helped me work through it."

"She doesn't think I'm a freak and demon to be put down?"

A smile ghosts across Eli's face. "No. She wasn't fond of you the first time she met you. You were pretty rude to her. But then she watched you while Dan was in the hospital. She saw the real you. Ava had no qualms about telling me I am an idiot for even thinking you're some monster waiting to spring to life on us."

He'd thought I was a monster? Even for a minute? That hurts.

"Mattie, I don't know what this thing between us is. It might be the bond making us feel like this. Or it might have enhanced our own feelings. I can't say. What I do know is I like you. A lot. Demon blood or not. I guess, what I'm trying to say…I'm still willing to give us a shot if you are."

"Eli, I grew up with people walking away from me, deciding I wasn't worth their time or effort because I was difficult. Sure, part of that was my fault, but even when I tried to be good, people still tossed me back. They always leave."

"But I didn't leave you, Mattie…."

"Yeah, Eli, you did. You walked away from me, from us, because I told you the truth about me. I threw my crazy at you, and you couldn't handle it. Who's to say when we find out what other crazy I have in me, it won't be worse than demon blood? Will you still stay, or will you book it?"

"I'm not going to bail again."

I look away. He says that, but when things get tough, who's to say he won't? Dan is the only person to never leave, to never walk out on me. He didn't care about my demon blood. I will guarantee even if he'd grown up like Eli and Caleb, it wouldn't have mattered. He would have stayed.

I don't know if I can say the same for Eli.

"Let's just get through dealing with Deleriel, and then we'll decide what to do about our feelings, okay?"

He gets up and leans over me, pulling my head back around to face him. His eyes are bright, brimming with unsaid emotion. "I am not leaving, Mathilda Louise Hathaway. If I have to prove that to you, then I will. But I'm not going anywhere."

His lips graze mine and that same warm feeling curls to life in the pit of my stomach that I get around him. It burns hot and fast, but I'm not ready to trust him quite yet. He does have to prove himself. I pull away from his kiss, and he sighs, but he doesn't argue with me.

"Fine, Hilda. I'll just have to prove it to you, then."

I lie back, feeling exhausted. My head has been pounding since Mary's visit, and dealing with Silas and Eli all in the same breath seems to have tuckered me out.

"I think I need a nap. Will you stay until Zeke and Dan get back?"

"Sure, sure." He settles back into the chair and props his feet up on the bed. "I could use a nap too."

My resolve softens the tiniest bit. He looks as exhausted as I feel. Instead of giving in and forgiving him, I close my eyes and let myself drift off to sleep.

***

The next time I wake up, I'm alone. Only the steady beeping of the machines to keep me company. Yawning, I sit up and shiver. I'm cold. Lila brought me one of those soft, fleecy throws, but I don't see it. The thing is warm, even able to dispel the chill from my bones. Where she got one in the dead of summer, I have no clue.

It's times like these I miss Eli. He gives off enough heat to warm me up, even from a distance. The one perk of his being my Guardian Angel is he's what I need him to be, and most times that's a living furnace.

It has to be late; it was nearly dark when I fell asleep. Starved. And I'm still starving. Did I miss dinner? Usually, they wake you up when they bring your tray of bland hospital food. My stomach is noisy enough I'd have eaten the nasty stuff just to get it to shush. Someone is going through a twenty-four-hour drive through if they let me sleep through dinner.

Zeke and Dan were supposed to bring me something from the cafeteria, though. A quick search of the room squashes that hope. Don't they realize my bottomless pit of a stomach needs to be fed?

The room still reeks of sulphur. It serves to remind me of Silas's visit. He left me with more questions than answers. Typical Silas. I don't know how to do what he wants me to, though. I did try, but I couldn't see past the surface of the man on his table. Even when I decided to draw him from memory, all I could see was his fear, his pain. I couldn't see the heart of him.

Silas knows how to do that. I'm sure of it. In order for me to deal with Deleriel, I need to understand what's under the surface of the façade he presents. I think that's what Silas has been trying to tell me all along. If I can do that, I'll be able to…I shake my head. I have no idea. I'm still sitting at go, no passing anything to collect the proverbial two hundred dollars.

I'm stuck. And I'm pretty sure there's only one way to get unstuck. I have to ask Silas for help. Zeke can't help me with this, and I don't trust Doc. I'm not sure I want him to either. Silas has always been adamant about me not telling him about my gift of bringing images to life.

While I don't think Zeke will hurt me or sacrifice me to gain more power, a small part of me wonders what he'd do if he knew what I could really do. There has to be a reason Silas doesn't want him to know. I laugh softly. Trusting a demon over my father. What a choice.

My door creaks open and I look up, ready to quarrel with Dan or Zeke about food, but it's neither of them standing there. Kayla Rawlins is standing in the soft glow of the bathroom light, her head tilted, watching me. Her eyes are yellow. The same color as the kid in the morgue.

Fear prickles along my skin. These little demon kids are dangerous. They feed on souls. No way is she getting near me. I look around for something to protect myself, but before I can do much, she shuffles into the room. Panic tries to crowd me, but I push it down. Now is not the time to panic.

She inches closer, and I see some of the damage that's been inflicted upon her poor body. Her yellow princess shirt is soaked through with blood, her white skirt not much better. She keeps stumbling, and I see her feet are twisted and broken, barely even attached to her legs anymore. The closer she gets, the more intense her eyes become, the yellow in them pulsing with a deep need.

Um, nope, not feeding on me. I scramble out of the bed, but the IV needle pulls painfully at my arm. I don't hesitate, I just rip it out. Same with all the little electrodes they have attached to my head and chest. I need to be able to move.

Dang it, she has me backed into a corner. There's no getting around her because she's standing between the foot of the bed and the wall. I pick up the brown tray under the water pitcher. Not that it'll do much good, but it's better than nothing.

"Stay right there, Kayla." I try to sound

as mean as I can without letting her know I'm scared.

She cocks her head and stares at me curiously. Does she recognize her name? Is there some part of the little girl I know left inside of the monster Deleriel created?

"Kayla, it's Mattie. You know me."

She keeps those yellow eyes fixed on me, and I try to slide a little closer to the bed. Maybe if I can jump over it, I can get around her? Not that I'm up to jumping. Just moving this little bit has caused my head to swim. Getting dizzy right now is not good.

She turns with me, and I stand still. Why hasn't she attacked?

Kayla puts a finger to her lips, the unspoken symbol to shush. Then she waves for me to follow her and shuffles toward the door. She pauses by the bathroom and looks to see if I'm behind her. She frowns, her yellow eyes blazing with irritation, but I see the fear behind it. She's terrified of something.

I take a few steps toward her, and she motions again for me to follow.

I shake my head to try to clear it. I'm dizzy, and now I'm getting blurry. Passing out is not a good idea. I can't protect myself from the little bugger trying to feed on me if I do.

But is following her any better? I have no idea where she wants to take me. It could be right back to that creepy little boy from my dream, Deleriel's first son. I hate when I end up in these horror movie scenarios. Door number one will get you killed, door number two will get you killed, and door number three will get you seriously killed.

Kayla opens her mouth and lets out this godawful keening that goes straight through my head, adding pain to my now perfect trifecta of passing out possibility. Door number three it is.

"Sheesh, kid, I'm coming. Stop it."

Her wail ceases, and I move forward, careful to hold onto what I can to keep from falling. Once I break the doorway, I see the nurses' station is empty. That would be the reason no one noticed the alarms going off on my machines when I pulled all the little electrodes off. Not sure if the IV machine has an alarm or not, or if there's still fluid leaking out of the needle. Probably a good thing no one is here. How to explain you're following a ghost so they don't try to suck your soul dry?

Yeah, no. Definitely would earn a visit from the psychiatrist on call.

Hospitals are creepy to begin with, but tonight this one is super creepy. None of the resident ghosts are out and about. I've had several pass through my room today, which I ignored completely. But they've all vamoosed. Another warning bell. Something is not right, but what else can I do?

The hallway is lit, but it seems to have some kind of shadow over it, like there's something here sucking all the light out of it. Maybe it's Kayla, I don't know, or maybe it's because my vision is blurring worse with every step I take. Either way, I don't like it.

Kayla pauses at the end of the corridor. She tilts her head, listening to something only she can hear. When she looks back at me, she's smiling. It's not a nice smile.

It's one full of teeth and intent. I take a startled step backward and fall into someone.

A squeal leaves my lips, and I bounce forward and away from whatever thing is behind me. "Mattie, stop."

Kane?

I turn my head to see the reaper who had been assigned to teach me. Kane's still dressed in the same clothes he always is, t-shirt and jeans. He must have died in those clothes. His black hair is messy, like he just rolled out of bed. He's cute for a reaper. Odd, I never noticed before. I'm not sure why I am now, while we're both in danger from the little demonic kid.

"Why are you following that thing?"

"Because it wanted me to?"

"Would you jump off a bridge too, if it asked?" The derision that rolls off his tongue sets my temper on fire.

"No, I would not. It was either follow it or suffer through some serious pain."

He snakes a glance at me. "Pain?"

"Worse than anything you can imagine."

"I doubt that. I died of a brain tumor. Now, that is some pain."

Kayla, growing frustrated, lets out another mind-numbing wail. Kane winces, and it's enough to make me fall, the pain flashing through my head so fast I can't get a grip on it. "Stop it!"

Kayla doesn't shush, and I struggle to stand. There's only one way she'll stop, and that's if I keep following her. Kane helps me to my feet, fussing that we should go back, but I can't. I have to follow her.

She leads us around the bend and opens the door to the stairwell. Kane leads me toward it. At least I'm not alone. "Hey, what are you doing here?"

"I felt the reaper in you rise up and call out. Your abilities are growing at an alarming rate if I could hear your call for backup."

"I did no such thing." I didn't, did I? Nope, I don't recall any such thing.

"You might not have realized it, but you did. I heard you, as did several others. They're here, watching, in case we need help." He throws a furtive glance at the kid. "And we might need help subduing one of Deleriel's creations."

There are other reapers here? I glance around, but they're not showing themselves. I shake my head then wince. I need to remember movement is bad when my head is aching like someone smashed it with a sledgehammer.

We follow her down three flights of stairs and into another empty hallway. Only it's not empty, really. It's full of construction equipment. CMC is adding a new pediatric wing to the hospital. Kayla's led us to there. At this time of night, there's no one around. We're alone with her.

"I don't think this is a good idea, Mattie," Kane whispers.

"Me either."

But we keep following her. She leads us down the hall and around the corner to where sheets of plastic cover the holes where the windows will go. They are flapping gently in the wind, adding to the eeriness of the hallway. The lighting down here is very dim, only a few lights flickering around us. The unearthly silence is deafening. Again, I wonder where the ghosts have fled to.

She enters the door in the middle of the hallway, and I start toward it, but Kane pulls me back. "Mattie, I think we should go back. Something is not right here."

"Yeah, I know, but we have to see what she's trying to show us."

"What if it's a trap? What if it's more of those kids than we can handle?"

"You said you brought backup, so we should be fine."

I start walking, and Kane is forced to continue since he's holding me steady. The floor is tilted and the walls are going round and round. It's making me sick to my stomach. I just hope I don't hurl on Kane. It's a distinct possibility, though.

The room in question is like any of the other ones down here, nothing special. It's just framing. They haven't even drywalled it yet. What makes this room unique is the little boy waiting for us. Deleriel's first child. I remember him distinctly from before. He's about seven or eight. His blond hair is stringy and matted with dried blood. Bruises cover him. His eyes, though, they are what keep your attention. He has no pupils. Instead, his entire eye is yellow. They are brimming with laughter tonight.

"Plaaay?"

"What is that thing?" Kane's whisper is even lower, and had he not been speaking right by my ear, I'd never have heard it.

"He's the first of Deleriel's children."

Kane sucks in a breath. His body trembles, and I can almost smell his fear. Yup, right there with him. This kid is scary.

He runs over to us, and I flinch away from him. He holds out his hand to me. "Plaaay?"

When I start to take it, Kane snatches it back. "What are you doing?"

"Finding out what he wants."

"Are you insane?"

"No, I'm not, Kane. I'm a living reaper. This is what I do, so let me do it."

He glares hot enough to scorch leather, but he doesn't argue.

I smile through my fear, determined to

do this. "I'm Mattie." He stares at me curiously. "What's your name?"

"Daaavviiid."

His voice is hoarse, drawn out. It's more of a hissing noise than anything resembling speech, but I understand him.

"Hello, David. Will you let me help you?"

He sticks his hand out further. "Plaaayy?"

I take his hand, half expecting Kane to stop me, but he doesn't. He's giving off waves of trepidation, though.

The little boy's hand is warm, not cold. All ghosts are cold, having lost everything that can give them the energy to generate heat. This kid, though, he's toasty warm. His fingers curl around mine, and he tugs me forward. I stumble, but right myself.

"Very, very good, my son."

My head whips up to see a figure in the corner. I hadn't seen him there before, but the room is full of shadows. He steps closer, under the light, and lets his hood fall back. I suck in a breath, not expecting the man who is staring at me. He's tall, with eyes the color of whiskey. Hair so blond, it's almost white enhances the color of his eyes. He's beautiful. That's the only word that comes to mind.

"Hello, Deleriel."

He smiles, and it's as if the angels themselves have smiled down upon me. It sends shivers across my skin.

"Hello, child." He moves closer, within a foot of me. "I was curious about you the day we met in the morgue. I caught your scent, and I knew who you were."

"You don't know anything about me." Silas said he doesn't know me. That I was protected, hidden.

"Oh, but I do, child, I do." He reaches a hand down to stroke the top of David's head. "My son likes you. Perhaps I shall let him play with you before we get down to business."

"Business?"

His smile widens into something that's not at all nice. "Yes, business. A deal was made, and I'm here to collect."

Crap on toast, he *does* know who I am.

"I made no deal with you, Deleriel."

"No, but your mother did. She

promised you to me."

"That deal is void." I keep my voice steady, calm, even though I might pee my pants, I'm so terrified.

"Void?" He lets out a surprised laugh. "How do you come by that conclusion, child?"

"She promised me to you, yes, but I'm not a child anymore. She can't consent to giving you my soul. It belongs to me. I'm the only one now who can give consent, and I'm not giving it to you."

"Very good, Emma Rose." He nods softly. "Silas has taught you well. Oh, yes, I knew he was hiding you. I have known from the day you were conceived. An inconvenience, and one I couldn't prove he had anything to do with. But that day in the morgue, I tasted you. You're a very distinct flavor. It was easy to find you after that. Ending up in this place of healing was fortunate. There are no wards or pesky guardians to deal with now. Just a lowly reaper who's cowering in the corner. I sent Kayla to you, knowing you'd follow my precious daughter, thinking you could help her in some way, the same as you offered David. It is in your nature to help these lost creatures."

"As it's yours to harm them."

"I saved them."

"By hurting them, by feeding off their pain and misery? You call that saving them? I call it sadistic."

His smile never falters, but the edge in his voice tells me I struck a nerve. "Watch your tongue, girl. You do not know of what you speak. My children, they adore me."

"Is that what you want? To be worshipped? Is that why you fell from grace?"

He chuckles. "Fell from grace? You watch too much television, child. I wanted more than I could gain in my position in Heaven. I've been quietly amassing power since I followed the Morning Star. Soon, I'll be ready to set up my own shop here on Earth. All I need is your soul to complete my arsenal. Then no one will be able to stop me."

"You can't have my soul, Deleriel. I will never give it to you. You can take me, you can torture me, you can do whatever you want, but you will not make me give up my soul."

"Even if I have something you want?" His voice turns cunning, reminding me so much of Silas.

"You don't have anything I could want."

"Oh, but I do, Emma Rose, I do." He steps forward and places his hand on my forehead. An image of Mary, alone in a room made of stone, floats into my line of sight. She looks scared. "You see, child? I do have something you want."

"You're lying."

"Am I?" He chuckles. "I will give you twenty-four hours to determine if I am lying. When I return, I will trade you her soul for yours."

Panic engulfs me, and I stumble backward, falling on my butt. Deleriel looms over me, smiling like a Cheshire cat. "It wouldn't do to have you die before you can give me your soul, now, would it?" He leans down and places a hand on my head. Warmth spreads like liquid fire through my entire body as healing energy floods every part of me.

Only it's not just healing energy I feel. I see so many things, I see a place foreign to me, beautiful and glorious. I see rolling hills flooded with bodies, broken and twisted wings a testament to the slaughter that took place. I see figures looming, whispering, judging. I see a dark and dangerous place, full of pain and death. Rage. I can taste rage and greed on my tongue. I see everything Deleriel was, is, and will be. I see it all.

The door in my mind opens, and I see *him*. I see past the mask he wears to the person beneath, the person he hides from everyone, even himself. I see the pain, the need for acceptance, the grief at losing everything he loved. I pity him, in a way.

When Deleriel pulls his hand away and looks down at me, he takes a startled step back. "What is this blasphemy?"

I sit up and rub my arms, feeling heat suffuse my body. It chases away the cold as I get to my feet. The pain is gone, and so is the dizziness.

"Mattie!"

Dan and Eli are both shouting my name. Deleriel looks toward the door. "I will return in twenty-four hours, and you will explain this blasphemy to me when I take your soul."

He disappears just as the two of them burst through the open doorway. They look around, wild-eyed, before their gazes settle on me. Dan speaks first. "Are you okay?"

"I'm fine. Better than fine." I crack my neck to dispel some of the stiffness. "But Mary's not."

"Mary?"

"Deleriel has Mary."

"How do you know that?" Eli keeps glancing to the spot Kane is standing in, silently watching, his eyes wide and worried.

"He showed me."

"Wait, he was here?" Eli asked. "No wonder my Spidey senses went all nuclear. Do you even realize the danger you were in?"

"I had backup."

"Backup?" Eli glances around again. "I don't see anyone else here."

"The reaper is here." Dan nods to Kane, who nods back.

"You can see the reaper?" Eli looks so confused. "Why can't I?"

"Because he's not bound to a living reaper the way you are, Daniel." Kane finally comes out of his daze and walks over to stand by us. "Eli will never be able to see me."

Dan repeats what Kane said, and Eli frowns, clearly not pleased. "That makes no sense. I'm bound to her too."

"Yes," Kane agrees. "He is, but he's her Guardian Angel. He can't see what you do, Mattie, but Daniel can because the angel bound his soul to yours. You shared your abilities with him, in a way. You remember the angel told you if he died, so did you, and vice versa? That is why Dan's been having nosebleeds and headaches. He's experiencing your symptoms to a certain degree. Not as bad, but had you died tonight, he would have too."

"I was going to die?" Really die?

"Had Deleriel not healed you, yes. Your body couldn't handle becoming a full-fledged reaper as it's trying to. We are working on a solution to this, but until we do, I can't promise you won't get sick again."

"Die?" Eli's face pales. "You're okay now?"

"I'm fine, but none of this is important. *He has Mary!*" Why are they not understanding how bad this is?

"Calm down, Hilda. Mary was just with us. We were over at Burger King. Caleb took her home, and I brought Dan back over here. You were passed out cold, so we went to grab some food. We even brought you back a double bacon cheeseburger and fries."

I ignore my stomach for once. "Call right now and make sure."

Dan pulls out his phone and calls his brother. It's a few rings before Caleb picks up. "Hey, Dan. Everything okay?"

"I don't know. Is Mary with you?"

"No, I dropped her off about half an hour or so ago. Why?"

"You have to go back to the house and make sure she's there," I blurt out. "Please, Caleb."

"What's going on?"

"Mattie thinks Deleriel took Mary." Dan doesn't sound like he believes me either.

"Have you called her?"

"No, but I will as soon as I hang up. Talk soon." Dan disconnects the call then pulls Mary's number up in his contacts, only this time the call goes straight to voicemail.

"Call the house phone." Mary knows to pay attention to the landline. It's the number her mother's work would call if they need to reach her. When Dan dials the number, it goes straight to voicemail as well.

"She's not there." Kane's somber voice interrupts us all. "I had one of our reapers go check. She's not at the house. There are signs of a struggle."

"See?" I screech. "I told you Deleriel has her.

Eli's phone rings and he pulls it out. "Mom?" He swipes his finger across the screen to answer it. "Hey, Mom."

"Eli, is your brother with you?"

There is no mistaking the panic in her

voice.

"No, Caleb is on his way to Mary's…"

"No, not Caleb, Benny."

"Benny?" Eli frowns. "No, I haven't seen him since this morning. What's going on, Mom?"

"I can't find your brother anywhere. I've searched the entire house, and Ava is out searching the block, but we can't find him, Eli."

Dan and I share a glance. No. They wouldn't dare take the child of an FBI agent who's already hunting them down.

Dan reaches for the phone, and Eli hands it over, dumbstruck, paralyzed with a fear so deep, I'm not sure how to help him.

"Heather? This is Dan. Call the police right now. Eli and I will be there shortly. Don't make any other calls before you dial 9-1-1. Do you understand?" He listens for a minute then nods, hanging up. "Mattie, we need to get you back to your room so I can drop Eli off at home then find out what's going on with Mary."

He leaves me to follow along behind

them as he grips Eli by the arm and leads him out of the room and back toward the stairwell.

My mind is a flurry of activities. Deleriel has Mary and Benny? That poor kid. I like him. I can't even imagine what Dan and Eli must be thinking.

Once back in our room, Dan calls Mr. Malone, and I try to comfort Eli, but he's inconsolable.

"What are we going to do?" He paces back and forth. "What are they doing to him right now? Oh, God, what's happening to my little brother?"

"Calm down, Eli. We'll find him."

"Will we?" he shouts. "We haven't found any of the other kids, and you know what their bodies looked like. What if...?"

"No." I stop him before he can go any further. "We will find him. I swear."

"You can't promise that, Mattie. You just can't."

But I can. "Silas!"

It takes only seconds for the demon to appear. It's as if he was waiting on my call.

"Hello, my darling girl."

"I need your help."

"And what will you give me for it?"

"Anything you want."

With his smile, my fate is sealed.

The End of Book 4

What do you think the missing piece of Mattie's heritage is? Tweet your response to me @AprylBaker using the hashtag #mattieis.

About the Author

So who am I? Well, I'm the crazy girl with an imagination that never shuts up. I LOVE scary movies. My friends laugh at me when I scare myself watching them and tell me to stop watching them, but who doesn't love to get scared? I grew up in a small town nestled in the southern mountains of West Virginia where I spent days roaming around in the woods, climbing trees, and causing general mayhem. Nights I would stay up reading Nancy Drew by flashlight under the covers until my parents yelled at me to go to sleep.

Growing up in a small town, I learned a lot of values and morals, I also learned parents have spies everywhere and there's always someone to tell your mama you were seen kissing a particular boy on a particular day just a little too long. So when you get grounded, what is there left to do? Read! My Aunt Jo gave me my first real romance novel. It was a romance titled "Lord Margrave's

Deception." I remember it fondly. But I also learned I had a deep and abiding love of mysteries and anything paranormal. As I grew up, I started to write just that and would entertain my friends with stories featuring them as main characters.

Now, I live in Huntersville, NC where I entertain my niece and nephew and watch the cats get teased by the birds and laugh myself silly when they swoop down and then dive back up just out of reach. The cats start yelling something fierce...lol.

I love books, I love writing books, and I love entertaining people with my silly stories.

Facebook:
https://www.facebook.com/authorAprylBaker

Twitter:
https://twitter.com/AprylBaker

Wattpad:
http://www.wattpad.com/user/AprylBaker7

Website:
http://www.aprylbaker.com/

Newsletter:
http://www.subscribepage.com/n0d6y8